Once again, for Geraldine,
My inspiration, without her this second book
would never have happened either

'Pak neee coodle toooo scoppp te nord matka.'

Dychweler erbyn y dyddiad olaf uchod
Please return by the last date shown

LLYFRGELLOEDD POWYS LIBRARIES

www.powys.gov.uk/llyfrgell
www.powys.gov.uk/library

disclaimer.
It should be noted that not one of the animals, insects or even plants mentioned in the stories were injured or badly treated during the writing of this book – apart from the wasp who was accidentally squashed between the last two pages just minutes before the book was sent to the printers…Oops! Sorry.

contents

1.

The clever clog.

'And what sort of present would you like me to buy you for your birthday young man?' said Granddad to little Poultice as he lifted him into the air and sat him on his lap.

'I would really, really love a great big television just like the one Nobby Pardon, who lives next door, has in his bedroom Granddad. Then I can watch the football as well,' replied Poultice smiling.

'Hmmmm,' said his Granddad, 'now that could be a little difficult as great big televisions are very, very expensive and your birthday is actually today. You are not giving me much time to save up my pension money are you?' he replied and laughed loudly.

'Anyway,' said Poultice's Grandfather waggling his finger 'you will never become a clever clogs if you are always watching the television.'

'Then if you can't afford to buy me a television I would like to be taller than I am now,' Poultice replied then added rather abruptly. 'That shouldn't cost you anything at all.'

'I don't think I could make you taller Poultice, especially not in just one day' replied his Grandfather. 'It would be a lot easier if you were to want something useful and something I could afford.'

'Then what about a nice thick book Granddad? I would find that useful and surely you could afford to buy one of those for me.'

Poultice's Granddad smiled, as he was so pleased at his Grandson's apparent interest in reading, learning and educating himself.

'I know just the book for you my lad, it's called an atlas and it has pages and pages of maps of all the countries in the whole wide world. It's a very large book indeed and so you must promise to make good use of it,' he added.

'I most certainly will Granddad. Your book will be the third I will own, and if it is an atlas it will also be the last one I will ever, ever need,' replied little Poultice.

'So what did your Mummy and Daddy buy you for your birthday?' enquired Poultice's Grandfather.

'Well, first of all I asked if they would buy me one of those great big televisions just like Nobby Pardon, who lives next door, has in his bedroom. They too said they were sorry but they just couldn't afford one, as they are far too expensive.

So I asked if they could make me taller and they told me exactly the same as you did, Granddad, that it was rather "short" notice for this year, but perhaps in a few years time.

So I then asked them to buy me a nice thick book instead and they certainly did, look!' and Poultice held the book up for his Grandfather to see.

Poultice's Universal Encyclopaedia was indeed one of the thickest books his grandfather had ever seen.

'They were so pleased with my choice of present Granddad. They hugged me and patted me on the head and told me that now I had an encyclopaedia I could become one of the brightest and cleverest young boys in the village!'

'That is excellent Poultice. Two books! My word' said Poultice's Grandfather.

'There's more Granddad, Uncle Curley called yesterday and also asked me what I would like for my birthday.

I told him I would like a great big television just like the one Nobby Pardon, who lives next door, has in his bedroom.

He told me as much as he would love to buy me one they are far too expensive and he just could not afford it.

So I thought I would ask Uncle Curley if he could make me taller.

He laughed out loud and said he would try his very best but it may take a good few years.

I told him that I didn't really have that much time, as it needed to be tomorrow at the very latest.

So I then asked Uncle Curley if he would buy me one of those big thick dictionary books that have the meaning of every word there is in it, and he did.

He even told me, that now I owned a dictionary I could easily become one of the brightest and cleverest young boys in the village.'

'Gosh Poultice you are a lucky boy,' said his Grandfather. 'You have a book that tells you the meaning of every word there is. You have a book that tells you about everything that has happened, not just on earth but also everywhere in the whole universe. You will even have a book that shows you the shape, size and whereabouts of every country in the entire world.

I think you are going to become clever. You have chosen three of the most interesting books ever written and you are correct, I don't think you will ever need any more books ever again.

So which one are you thinking of reading first?' enquired Poultice's Grandfather.

'Well I don't intend to read any of them,' replied Poultice.

'You see, first of all I am going to put your big thick atlas on the floor next to the radiator in my bedroom.

Then, I will place the encyclopaedia that Mum and Dad bought me on top of it.

After that I will carefully place the big thick dictionary that Uncle Curley bought me on top of both of them.

Then, if I am very, very careful, I can climb to the top and when I stand up straight I will be as tall as I ever want to be.

In fact I will be so tall I will be able to see right into Nobby Pardon's bedroom and I can watch the football match on **his** great big television!'

'I have the feeling,' muttered Poultice's Grandfather shaking his head slowly, 'you may well already be the cleverest clog in the village...'

The end

2.

A brilliantly
great idea indeed.

Now, if there was one thing in the whole world that Scunthorpe the sparrow really, really wanted to do, it was to open his very own shop...

'I have been thinking,' trilled Scunthorpe one Monday morning to Wexley, his very best friend, 'what about opening a café?'

'I think a café would be a brilliantly great idea Scunthorpe, ' replied Wexley. 'On the top most branch of one of the tallest trees in the woods would be peaceful, and there would be some lovely views as well,' squawked Wexley.

'Don't you think that near some other shops would be ideal?' trilled Scunthorpe.

'Close to something interesting or sporty would be lots of fun,' the two sparrows chirped together and laughed out loud, the way sparrows always tend to do when they chirp exactly the same thing at exactly the same time.

'We are going to need a catchy name and I think we should have something really special outside the front door just to attract the customers,' added Scunthorpe. Wexley nodded in agreement.

It was late one spring evening when the two friends were returning home from work when they just happened to see exactly what Scunthorpe had been looking for.

It was an old wooden birdhouse hanging from one of the lower branches of a beech tree at the bottom of a garden which, would you believe it, was as close as close could be to a football ground.

A small family of robins, who used it to sell wrapping paper, crackers and tinsel at Christmas time, had only just vacated the little birdhouse. One of the robins had earned so much from having his photograph printed on Christmas cards that they had decided to save up and buy a large nest with a swimming pool out in Spain where the weather was so much warmer.

The house did need a little bit of work to tidy it up. A good sweeping inside and a coat of paint on the walls, but it was exactly what Scunthorpe had been looking for.

'I would like to call it 'The Bird's Café', tweeted Scunthorpe proudly. 'Whenever there is a game at the football ground it will be full of other birds wanting a quick snack and a drink before they fly over to the ground to watch the match from high up in the rafters of the stands.'

Wexley nodded in agreement. 'A brilliantly great idea Scunthorpe,' and he flapped his wings and whistled a little football song.

The café had a black felt roof and a pretty yellow chimney. The walls were all painted red on the outside and it made the café look as though there were real windows with blue-striped curtains. In the wall at the front there was a round hole that would allow all the birds in to eat and when they had finished, it would allow them back out again.

The two sparrows spent week after week painting, cleaning, and tidying. They made little tables and chairs out of sticks and twigs that they found lying on the ground.

Finally they added two big signs, a catchy one above the door that read:

> **THE BIRD'S CAFÉ**
> **Treat yourself to a tweet.**

And the other, just under the window that said:

> **Reopening – Under New Management.**
> **Everybirdy Welcome.**

'Hmmmm, I'm not quite sure if that is going to be quite cute enough to attract the customers,' squawked Wexley.

'I think we ought to do something extra special on the first day we open,' tweeted Scunthorpe, 'and I have been thinking about one of those "eat as much as you like for almost nothing" days, just as a sort of "special opening" offer.'

'That sounds like a brilliantly great idea,' chirped Wexley. 'In fact, there is a game being played on Saturday. What if we were to make

Saturday our opening day?'

'An even better most brilliantly great idea' Scunthorpe chuckled, but Wexley failed to see the funny side of his joke.

'Hey, pardon what?' replied Wexley scratching his head with his wing.

They immediately started to think about a menu for the food.

They decided they would offer customers the usual worms and grubs as well as some of those tasty little flying insect things you sometimes catch fresh in the summer but were now available frozen in boxes from a shop in town called 'Greenland'.

Wexley even suggested they should have seeds and breadcrumbs as well, just in case some of the birds were vegetarians.

Saturday morning arrived and the little café quickly began to fill with customers.

There were birds of all descriptions chirping and tweeting, whistling and singing and eagerly discussing which team they thought was going to win the match.

Scunthorpe and Wexley were bustling around doing their best to serve everyone with whatever food or drinks they fancied.

'The wrens on table one would like five worms, the starlings on table seven fancy a bowl of our juiciest grubs with seeds, and the big crow on table twelve wants one more kebab and another plate of cheesy chips,' squawked Wexley to Scunthorpe who was busy in the kitchen out the back.

The Bird's Café was indeed chirping with activity.

It was getting very close to the time for the match to start when Wexley's rather worried face peered through the door into the kitchen.

'Erm, I think we might have an itsy bitsy problem out here Scunthorpe,' he tweeted.

'That big crow at table twelve who had the kebabs, with a side order of onion rings and two plates of cheesy chips has become stuck in the door and no-one can get pass him and go to the match.'

It was true the greedy black crow had eaten so much food he was now bigger than the little doorway he came in through and in trying to get out had become stuck fast. Some of the other birds tried pulling and pushing at his tail, but he just would not budge. 'What are we going to do Scunthorpe?' cried Wexley. 'There is only fifteen minutes before kick off and no-one can get out.'

Scunthorpe sat down and thought.

'Just a minute,' he squawked, 'I remember the robins who lived here telling me that if ever Father Christmas needed extra paper for wrapping some late presents on Christmas Eve, he would always come into the shop down the chimney, just for practice I suppose. Perhaps we can get everyone out through there.'

'Another brilliantly great idea,' squawked Wexley, and he shouted out some instructions to all the birds in the café.

'I think we may all have eaten a little too much today Scunthorpe,' chirped one of the wrens, 'and we are just not quite slim enough to even get out through the chimney. What are we going to do?'

Scunthorpe sat down once again and thought.

'Just a minute,' he squawked, 'I remember Linford the racing pigeon telling me the other day that if you want to lose a few centimetres from around your waist then the best way to do it is exercise. So, five minutes of running on the spot and twenty press-ups everyone,' shouted Scunthorpe. 'By then you all should be that little bit slimmer and fit into the chimney.'

'Yet another brilliantly great idea,' whistled Wexley loudly and he started jogging on the spot just to show the other birds what to do.

Scunthorpe was right, just five minutes exercising and virtually every bird in the café had lost enough weight to be able to squeeze themselves up through the little yellow chimney and out onto the roof.

Everyone arrived at the stadium just in time for kick off. That is with the exception of the big black greedy crow. He was still stuck fast in the front doorway.

'Shall I fly over to the forest and fetch the woodpeckers, Scunthorpe? They can chip away at the wood and set him free.'

Scunthorpe sat down once again and thought.

'No, why don't we leave him there, it will stop any more greedy crows getting in and you must admit that from the outside he does give the front of the café that sort of special look we have been searching for.'

Scunthorpe was correct. Flocks of birds visited the café for something to eat and for something to drink, and to laugh at the greedy black crow that was stuck fast in the doorway.

'A brilliantly great idea indeed,' chirped Scunthorpe and Wexley, both at the same time, and they laughed out loud, the way sparrows tend to do when they say exactly the same thing, at exactly the same time.

The end

3.
Caswell gets
a certificate.

Caswell was a very old, dark oak mantle clock that sat on the top of a writing desk in the living room of Mr. Chuddlewick's cottage in the little village of Tipton Down in Thropshire. He was indeed a beautiful wooden clock. He had a very loud tick and an equally loud tock. Everyone that visited Mr. Chuddlewick's cottage would always say how bright and shiny he looked and how loud and clear he always chimed.

Every Sunday morning, at exactly ten o'clock, Mr. Chuddlewick would wind Caswell's curly black spring exactly six turns of the key. Then he would clean his brass face and polish and buff his wooden case.

Caswell enjoyed Sundays and loved being wound up.

'It's, it's, it's like being tickled with a feather,' he would tell all the other pieces of furniture in the room, long after Mr. Chuddlewick had gone to bed, of course.

He especially loved being cleaned and polished. It was so relaxing that sometimes it made him fall asleep and, would you believe it... stop! He had a large round brass face with '**CASWELL**' printed near the bottom in a very slight curve that made it look as though he was actually smiling. He had twelve different numbers made up of 'Is', 'Vs' and 'Xs' that were placed at precise intervals all around the outside of his shiny brass face.

Caswell also had two black hands. One was very long and slender and one rather short and stubby and both went slowly around and around his face throughout the day and all through the night, pointing and telling anyone who needed to know exactly what time it was, and it was exactly that time.

Not only was Caswell the shiniest clock in the whole of Thropshire, but he was also the most accurate as well.

Mr. Chuddlewick loved his clock more than anything else in the whole wide world, but there was one tiny little problem that had Mr. Chuddlewick very concerned indeed.

Caswell was never quite sure how many times he had to chime.

Mr. Chuddlewick thought because the clock was so old, after all Caswell was one-hundred-and-one last February, that he might have forgotten how to count.

Sometimes, when it was three o'clock in the afternoon, he would chime eight times.

Then sometimes, when it was ten o'clock in the morning, he would only chime twice.

Twelve o'clock was the most difficult time of all for Caswell to try and get right. Once, just once, he was almost correct but chimed thirteen times instead of twelve and then decided to chime thirteen times again because he was not sure how many chimes he had chimed the first time. Chiming twenty-six times not only confused Mr. Chuddlewick but confused all the other pieces of furniture in the room as well.

'I am beginning to think that you need to go back to school Caswell,' he would mutter to himself whilst rubbing his chin.

Caswell would always try his very best but no matter how hard he tried he never ever managed to chime the same number that his little hands were pointing towards.

'It's easy for Mr. Chuddlewick; although he has the same number of hands as I have he has five fingers on each one of them so counting is simple. I don't have any fingers on either of my hands, and as well as that I am also one-hundred-and-one years old. Surely I'm far too old to go back to school,' Caswell told the other pieces of furniture in the room, long after Mr. Chuddlewick had gone to bed, of course.

There is something quite strange about wooden furniture that not many people know. Tables, chairs and even sideboards never ever go to sleep until well after people have gone to bed. It's the time they enjoy most when they can talk to each other, tell a couple of jokes and discuss the various happenings that have occurred during the day. So because they are very late going to sleep in the night they are always the last to wake up the following morning. In fact they will not wake up until well after everyone in the house is either gone to school or to work.

It was about ten o'clock one Monday morning when the table yawned loudly and noticed that Caswell wasn't in his usual place on the top of the writing desk.

'Has anyone seen Caswell?' he asked.

'I think I heard him chime six times at nine o'clock and then Mr. Chuddlewick picked him up and put him into a big brown leather bag,' replied the sideboard.

'Perhaps he has been taken back to school,' gasped one of the chairs rather nervously, 'he is not going to like that.'

It was just after seven o'clock in the evening when Mr. Chuddlewick returned home carrying his big brown leather bag. He carefully lifted Caswell out and placed him back in his usual position on top of the writing desk.

Caswell looked brighter and cleaner than he had ever looked before, and he started to tick and tock as though he had never ever been away.

Later that evening, as soon as Mr. Chuddlewick had locked all the doors, turned off all the lights and went to bed, Caswell told his friends all about his day at school. He told them about the other clocks that were in the same classroom, about the ones that could tick but couldn't tock and some that would tock loudly and then just stop.

'There were some there that didn't even know how to chime,' he added, and all the furniture in the room gasped in astonishment.

'I have learnt how to count up to twelve and I know how to chime once at half past every hour, although I still don't quite understand why I need to do it. I can understand multiplying and dividing and I can solve really difficult quadratic equations as well,' Caswell announced proudly and the smile on his face became even wider.

'I learned quite a lot at school, in fact before we left to come home I think I saw the teacher give Mr. Chuddlewick a certificate to say I had passed.'

'A certificate, Caswell has a *certititititifficate!!!!!!!!*' they all added in surprise and even the drawers on the sideboard opened wide in astonishment.

'I wish I had a certititititificate,' said the writing desk. 'Perhaps Mr. Chuddlewick will send me back to school. Although I am a writing desk I don't ever remember having been taught how to write. Would you teach me how to write, Caswell, now that you have been back to school and studied for one of those *certititititititificates.*'

'I can certainly try tomorrow,' replied Caswell, 'but at this moment I need to concentrate as I have to make my first twelve o'clock chime.'

It was just before midnight when eventually they all stopped talking and looked across at the brightly-polished clock sitting on top of the writing desk.

At precisely twelve o'clock Caswell chimed exactly twelve times, and a big grin spread across his shiny, brass face.

All the other pieces of furniture in the room clapped and cheered loudly, but not loud enough to wake Mr. Chuddlewick, of course.

Not very many people have ever heard wooden furniture clap and cheer loudly because at that time of night most of them are fast asleep.

The end

4.

Tilly Fragglehurst
saves the world.

Everyone in Clodborough knew Tilly Fragglehurst. In fact, if truth were to be told, everyone in the whole wide world knew of Tilly Fragglehurst.

Tilly was a top quality grizzler. Best in the world, according to some.

She could always find something to moan about. She once won an Olympic Gold Medal at grizzling, or so the story goes.

Strange though it may seem, Tilly had never said anything about that to anyone, as though she had forgotten it or didn't know about it at all.

One of her favourite grizzles was always the weather.

If it rained, Tilly would grumble that the rain was too wet.

If ever the wind blew, even the slightest puff, Tilly would whinge that the wind was blowing too noisily and it was always blowing in her direction.

Even if it were warm and sunny, Tilly would grouse that it was too hot and the sun was shining far too brightly. She would moan bitterly and even suggested there should be a little knob or even a button somewhere she could twist or press to turn the sunshine down.

Tilly complained about everything. She even grumbled about the milkman because his bottles clacked together rather noisily when they were empty.

But the best, and daily, grizzle of all was always about Percy Twinkle, the postman, because he was always too slow and never posted the letters through her box quietly enough.

She even groused about the children who lived in Clodborough. They could never ever do anything right, according to Tilly.

She would complain whenever she saw them kicking a ball. When she caught them whispering she would first tell them it was rude and then moan at them for talking too quietly.

Once she even grumbled when she saw Redfern Pocklebank picking his nose.

'You make sure that goes into a bin young lad,' she told him rather sternly and waggled her finger at him. 'We don't want anyone tripping or slipping on it now do we?' she added and continued to moan as she took Redfern all the way home to make sure he put the little boggie in the wastebin.

Redfern's sports teacher was not at all happy because Redfern was playing in goal for the school football team at the time and they ended up losing the match twenty-six goals to nil. Their worse defeat ever. Tilly Fragglehurst cared not one jot.

As a result, Tilly Fragglehurst was known to everyone in the whole wide world as 'Miss Grizzleaddictum.'

Nobody, however, let Tilly in on the secret.

There was just one person in Clodborough that Tilly never ever grizzled about, and that person was herself. Tilly was always right and did nothing wrong at all.

She lived on her own in a little cottage called Number Eleven at the very end of Troglodyte Street in Clodborough. There were ten other cottages in the same street but nobody lived in them. They had all moved away to countries like New Zealand, Argentina or Russia because Tilly would grizzle and moan then moan and grizzle at them all day long.

It was almost nine o'clock one warm summer's evening when suddenly the kitchen light in Number Eleven Troglodyte Street began to glow brighter and brighter and then, when it was as bright as bright could be, it glowed even brighter still.

'What on earth is going on?' Tilly whinged to herself as she looked out through the kitchen window and saw, first to her surprise and then to her dismay a rather large silver-coloured, saucer-shaped spaceship, which had just landed right in the middle of her precious and luscious green lawn.

'I'll soon put a stop to this,' she groused to herself and grabbed her big black umbrella, from the coat stand in the hall, before opening the kitchen door and storming angrily into the garden.

The silver spaceship suddenly began to pulse and hum, sending sporadic pencil beams of coloured laser lights all across the front of Tilly's little cottage.

A loud creaking and grating sound could be heard from beneath the four slender legs of the silver craft, and, slowly but surely, a door began to lower itself towards the ground.

Out of the thick smoky mist that oozed from the open door appeared five rather strange looking creatures. They each had three eyes, one at the front and one on each side of their lumpy white heads, which were of a shape that reminded Tilly of cycling helmets. Each one had two short stubby legs and four extremely long arms at the end of which were three spiny fingers with short blue nails that looked, to Tilly, as though they had been bitten.

'Disgusting habit,' muttered Tilly

'Get that silly looking contraption off my lawn at once,' Tilly grumbled loudly and pointed with her umbrella, 'look at the dents it is making in my grass. You ought to be ashamed of yourselves making all that smoke. And that light is far too bright for my liking as well. Switch it off immediately.'

'*Splot plitch dnok fooble?*' questioned one of the aliens who had black razor sharp teeth, a rather large, wet nose that continued to dribble, and the word 'Kevin' written in pink on the front of his space suit.

'*Wagant diddy bloop Yadak,*' replied the one standing next to him who had an even larger and wetter nose but it didn't dribble quite as much as Kevin's.

A long, thin, cold, clammy arm suddenly appeared from the back of the little gathering and slowly, with the middle finger extended, made its way towards Tilly's grim and sour face.

'How dare you point your finger at me,' shouted Tilly, and she struck the back of the creature's hand a hefty blow with the handle of her umbrella.

'Don't you know it's rude to point?' she gruffed. 'You need to be taught some manners young man.'

The creature squealed loudly and the hand quickly disappeared behind the rest of the group.

'*Pak neee coodle toooo scoppp te nord matka*,' bellowed Kevin just as Tilly's umbrella struck him across the top of his rather long white head.

'Speak when you are spoken to and not before!' said Tilly.

'*Yeeeeeeek!*' screamed the alien as some rather thick and gooey green slime dribbled from his nose onto the garden path, splogging just in front of Tilly's foot.

'And you can mop that up before you go any further!' she added and poked and prodded the creature with the end of her umbrella until he did exactly what Tilly had told him to.

The five aliens were certainly taken by surprise and huddled together to discuss what to do next.

'*Bibba duckle toop!*' shouted one of them suddenly, and they all gasped in astonishment before once again turning their heads to look at Tilly. All five pointed their long thin fingers in her direction and uttered in perfect English, '*Tilly Fragglehurst, Olympic Gold Medal Winner.*'

'Well yes it is Tilly actually,' she answered rather pleased that someone or something even if they were from another planet, actually knew her name. 'But hey, what's that you said about a gold medal?'

'*Oh, poddle!*' said the one called Kevin as he shook his hand-held galactic navigation system rather vigorously until a number of springs, cogs and screws rattled and fell out onto the ground. '*This must be Earth, we have invaded the wrong planet!*' exclaimed Kevin looking once more at his galactic navigator now that he had managed to replace the springs and cogs.

The other four aliens gasped in dismay and smacked Kevin on the back of his head with each of their hands, making sixteen smacks in all.

Tilly made sure all the marks on the lawn were removed and all the flowers that were bent when the spaceship landed were straightened before she allowed them to leave.

Tilly continued grizzling until the spaceship door finally closed. Kevin even apologised and promised they would never ever return to Earth.

The next morning when Percy Twinkle the postman arrived with Tilly's mail, she related to him the story about the five aliens who had landed on her lawn the previous night, flattening her grass and bending all her flowers.

'But there are no marks on the grass Miss Fragglehurst and all the flowers are still standing up perfectly straight,' remarked Percy Twinkle. 'I can only assume they must have been very careful in case you complained at them.'

'What?' grizzled Tilly, 'I have never had reason to complain about anyone in my whole life and so there would be no point in starting now,' she added rather gruffly.

'Anyway, what do you think about this?' and Tilly held up a rather large gold medal attached to a long length of multicoloured ribbon. 'I found it on the lawn just as the spaceship left. They must have dropped it.'

'It has "**Winner - Miss Grizzleaddictum**" marked on it. Who do you think it could belong to?'

'Let me see,' said Percy Twinkle rubbing his chin, and trying hard not to laugh, as he pretended to give the question some considerable thought.

'Miss Grizzleaddictum! Hmmm, nope, nothing springs to mind. I can't think of anyone by that name around Clodborough and I have been the postman for almost fifty years.'

'Good, in that case I will keep it, it will look nice on my mantelpiece,' said Tilly, 'now off my lawn please Mr Twinkle and be on your way. You have been standing there so long your feet are beginning to flatten my grass.'

'Yes Miss Fragglehurst,' said Percy, as he made his way down the garden path.

'And don't slam the gate.'

'No Miss Fragglehurst,' said Percy.

'And don't walk on the gravel. I can't stand that crunching sound,' Tilly added as she watched the postman carefully make his way back to the post office.

'Yes Miss Grizzle...oops! I mean no Miss Fragglehurst.'

'What did you just call me Mr. Twinkle?'

'Mr. Twinkle??'

'Mr. Twinkle???' Tilly kept shouting from the gate.

Percy Twinkle was almost halfway back to the post office by then.

It's amazing how quick a postman can deliver mail when he knows someone is going to complain or grizzle at him.

The end

5.
The race.

'Here they come again, it's the third year on the trot they have entered the race and I don't know why they bother,' said Wilfred one of the race organisers shaking his head in total disbelief. 'What do they call themselves, TEAM LOS AMIGOS or something,' he added and chuckled loudly. 'They made such a mess of the whole event over the last two years you would think that by now they would have learnt a lesson and given up.'

It was true, the annual 'Once Around The Garden' team race for snails (all categories) was only supposed to take a weekend but last year Orson, Ibstock and Chepstow or TEAM LOS AMIGOS, as they preferred to be known, got lost and Wilfred, quite late on a Sunday night, had to organise a search party to go and look for them.

He was not amused at all

They were eventually found next to a plastic tub of ginger beer in the middle of a bed of French marigolds singing some old Elvis Presley songs at the tops of their voices whilst doing their very best to empty the tub of its ginger beer using a straw that Orson had found on the grass near a barbeque.

'Wait a minute, wait a minute what's all this?' bellowed Wilfred pointing at a rather strange contraption perched on the top of Orson's shell.

'It's a roof rack,' answered Orson, 'instead of carrying our food and blankets around in suit cases, our tent, picnic table, chairs and lettuce leaves will all be stored up there for the race. We think we should be able to travel twice as fast as we did last year.'

'Well what has he got on his shell?' spluttered the bewildered Wilfred as he looked towards Ibstock.

'It's called a spoiler and he has been race testing it all summer,' said Orson. 'Now that he has set the angle correctly he has even managed to shave 0.15 of a second off his best one centimetre sprint times. So he will be faster too.'

It was true. Ibstock had fitted a bright red spoiler to his shell similar to one he had seen on a Ferrari. It had nearly run him over as he was crossing the road when returning from the churchyard early one Thursday morning after prayers.

'And that other idiot,' added Wilfred in total disbelief, 'what on earth is that thing sticking out in front of his face?'

'Ah! Now that is our "secret weapon" you are looking at,' sniggered Chepstow. 'It's the latest state of the art satellite navigation system. I only had it fitted last week. It is virtually impossible for us to get lost once I twist this switch.

The salesman at Halfords said it's really easy to use as well, you press these buttons here to tell it where you are, and then you press those buttons there to tell it where you want to go. It shows you pictures of the route and exactly where you need to turn whether it is right or left. Accurate to the nearest centimetre, according to the instruction leaflet. So this year expect to see us on the finish line long before anyone else arrives,' added Chepstow and the two other team members nodded smuggly in agreement.

'Roof racks, spoilers, and satellite navigation, I have never known anything like it in all my life. I have been running this race for well over ten years you know, and this has never ever happened before. In fact, as I am the race organiser, the three of you are disqualified,' said Wilfred rather sternly and he started to slither across the grass towards the start line where at least twenty other teams were eagerly waiting for someone to shout the word "GO".

'Where in the rule book does it say you can't use roof racks, spoilers or sat nav systems?' enquired Chepstow.

'Here, look,' replied Wilfred and he held up a little black book for Chepstow to see.

'The ink is still wet, you must have just written that rule in when you turned your back on us,' said Chepstow.

'Ok, perhaps I did,' replied Wilfred, 'but I have been meaning to add it in for some time. As all the other teams are ready to start I am going to let you three back into the race, but don't let it happen again.'

Twenty-one teams with three snails in each waited behind a rather silvery line that Wilfred had laid down on the path earlier that morning.

'**Ready... Steady... GO!**' yelled Wilfred and he raised his little white handkerchief high into the air.

'**Stoooooooop**,' yelled Wilfred and he tucked his little white handkerchief under his shell.

'That was a false start, everyone back behind the lines, the kid with that stupid red spoiler moved.'

'No I didn't, replied Ibstock, 'I just sneezed that's all.'

'I don't care, according to the rules that's still classified as a move,' replied Wilfred pointing to something written on another page in his little black book.

'TEAM LOS AMIGOS are penalised. They can't start for another hour because they moved before the word **GO**,' he announced loudly to all the other competitors. 'Look, it says so here in my rules book,' and he waved it frantically in the air.

'He's trying to get the ink to dry that's why he waving it about,' said Orson. 'I bet he has only just written that rule as well.'

TEAM LOS AMIGOS watched as all the other snails jostled for positions along the path that led down towards the garden shed. I was the first leg of the race.

'Don't worry,' said Chepstow confidently 'we have all the technical wizardry to assist us which means that we will be at the finish line long, long before any of the other teams.'

Chepstow was correct. TEAM LOS AMIGOS were at the finish line on that Sunday afternoon well before any one of the other twenty teams.

They didn't win though, they didn't even come second, and in fact they didn't even come last.

Wilfred smugly announced that, 'TEAM LOS AMIGOS are disqualified because they failed to finish.'

You see, when Chepstow pressed the buttons on his sat nav stating precisely where they were and then pressed the other buttons on the sat nav to state precisely where they wanted to go both places turned out to be exactly the same.

The start and finish line.

So, for two days TEAM LOS AMIGOS never actually moved.

'I still think we sort of won,' said Ibstock.

'We were definitely at the finishing line before anyone else,' said Orson.

'Ah well, better luck next year then,' said a rather disappointed Chepstow.

'Plot us a course for home Chepstow,' said Orson.

'Can't, batteries have gone flat,' replied Chepstow.

'Oh! Now that's a bit of a bummer lads,' said Wilfred, with a big beaming smile as he slowly made his way home across the grass.

He stopped, thought for a moment, and then turned around.

'Wait a minute, did I just hear one of you say next year?' and the big beaming smile slowly began to disappear off Wilfred's face.

The end

6.

The rise and fall of Fedwink Rumblebutt.

Standing in the middle of a large yellow cornfield in front of Farmer Wicklow's barn was a rather strange looking figure.

He was dressed in a faded dark grey suit, the sleeves of which were covered with small holes. There were three large rusty buttons down the front of his jacket and a length of string holding it tightly around his waist.

Beneath the jacket he wore a shirt, which, probably once upon a time was whiter than white but had, over the years, become rather stained, drab and a little colourless.

On his head he wore a small blue hat with a faded pink coloured ribbon around the middle, which fluttered and waved in the air every time the wind blew.

His face was a rugged sandy brown, well weathered, and he had a large round nose right in the very middle of it.

Two dark black eyes stared forward never closing, never blinking, and never, for that matter, looking from side to side.

It was Fedwink Rumblebutt.

It was Fedwink's job to make sure that the Crows, the Sparrows and other countryside birds never stole the seeds that Farmer Wicklow planted in the field.

Fedwink was a scarecrow.

He had worked all his life on the farm and loved it. He started with a sort of apprenticeship as a handle to one of Farmer Wicklow's booms but then, one day, when the farmer's wife needed a wooden prop for her clothesline, the Farmer offered Fedwink the job.

Or so Feswink told everyone.

Propping up the farmer's wife's clothesline was a very difficult job indeed.

'One needs exceptional balance and poise!' claimed Fedwink who thought of himself as one of the more important members of the 'domestic' staff at the farm.

Fedwink was very ambitious and always looking for other jobs on the farm he could try his hand at.

One particular day he heard Farmer Wicklow telling his wife he needed a scarecrow to look after the newly planted seeds in the cornfield, and Fedwink decided it was just the sort of job he would like to do. So he applied for it.

Or so Fedwink told everyone.

Fedwink was the only scarecrow on the farm and, as a result, he considered his move from 'domestic assistant' in the laundry department to 'head of external security' as a major rise in status.

He was extremely proud when the Farmer gave him a nearly new dark grey suit to wear.

The suit jacket even had three shiny buttons down the front.

Beneath his jacket he wore the brightest white shirt you have ever seen and on his head a blue hat with a bright red ribbon for a band that fluttered and waved every time the wind blew.

Fedwink loved his job as 'head of external security' so much he would stay out in the field all day and all night, through wind and rain and sometimes even snow.

Over four years passed by and Fedwink still enjoyed his work, in fact he enjoyed it so much that he never ever moved from the very same spot in the very same field.

His hat had blown off once or twice during rather windy nights but he still stood proud and tall, guarding the farmer's corn.

There was, however, one itsy, bitsy problem with being a scarecrow. Scarecrows really need to scare the Crows or, for that matter, any birds.

Fedwink, unfortunately, just didn't really like scaring the birds. They were all friends of his and he enjoyed listening to them chatter, chirp and sing from dawn until dusk

During the day he would stretch his arms out wide, not to frighten the birds away, but to give them somewhere to perch, feed on the corn and generally chatter amongst themselves.

Farmer Wicklow, however, did not like to see any birds at all sitting on Fedwink's arms or on top of his head and he would do his very best to frighten them off.

'That's the third time the farmer has looked out of his kitchen window' chirped Statistic, the little House Sparrow. 'Do you remember what happened last time Fedwink?' he added.

At that moment, from an upstairs window of the farmhouse, came one of the loudest bangs you have ever heard in your life, followed just a few seconds later by another, which was probably even louder than the first. The birds sitting on Fedwink's arms scattered in all directions, squawking and screeching and flapping their wings as fast as ever they could.

'Yipes!' cried Fedwink as a cloud of smoke rose from the end of two long steely grey gun barrels that the farmer was pointing in his direction.

'Ouch! Ouch! Ouch!' Bellowed the scarecrow. Then, 'Ouch! Ouch! Ouch! He bellowed once again as nasty little pellets from the farmer's shotgun made hole after hole, first in the left hand sleeve of his jacket and then in the right.

'Phew, that was close,' said Bakewell the Bullfinch as he settled on the branch of a nearby tree.

'One of them missed me by just two point five centimetres,' added Statistic, the little House Sparrow.

Total silence had suddenly fallen on the cornfield.

The silence didn't last very long though and within a few minutes the birds were back perched on Fedwink's arms and head squawking and whistling at the tops of their voices as if nothing had ever happened. 'I don't like being shot at' said Fedwink rather sadly. 'Perhaps it's time I started to look for a better job?'

It was late in the evening when Statistic looked at his watch and pointed out to the other birds that not only was nine o'clock fast approaching but also Farmer Wicklow was rumbling across the field towards them on his bright Red Forden Tractor.

'Good night Fedwink' chirped the birds as they left their perches on Fedwink's arms for their nests in the nearby trees.

'Good night' said Fedwink. 'See you all again tomorrow morning.'

The following morning was so warm the sun decided to rise even earlier than usual.

'Wake up, wake up everyone' chirped a rather agitated Statistic. 'I have some terrible news. Fedwink has disappeared. All that's left is a hole in the ground about a metre in width and sixty centimetres deep. He is nowhere to be seen.'

The birds gasped in disbelief.

It was true. In the spot where Fedwink had stood for over four years there was indeed a hole in the ground, a metre in width and sixty centimetres deep, exactly as Statistic had said.

In fact the only clue that Fedwink had ever been there at all was an almost colourless pink ribbon lying motionless on the ground. It didn't even flutter when the wind blew.

'A sad, sad day indeed' chirped Bakewell the Bullfinch, and all the other birds nodded in agreement.

It was some days later when, Statistic, the little sparrow, squawked excitedly as he flew back towards the trees.

'I've seen him, I've seen him!' he chirped. 'I've seen Fedwink. He's alive and well and even has a new job on the farm.'

Sure enough, there to everyone's surprise, high above the roof of the barn was Fedwink. Attached to the end of his left arm he had a large silver television aerial and attached to the end of his right arm he had one of those new fangled black Sky satellite dishes.

'Well I never!' squawked all the birds in unison.

'And look' chirped Statistic as he used his special little tape measure, 'there is still thirty five point six centimetres on either side where we can all sit and chat.'

'So what happened Fedwink?' chirped Buxton the Blackbird.

'Well,' answered Fedwink thinking very hard for a reason as to why he had suddenly re-appeared fixed to the roof of the barn. 'You see when Farmer Wicklow arrived on his tractor the other evening he told me he needed his best suit back. He also told me there was an even better job on the farm, which he thought I might be interested in. He even promised I wouldn't be shot at ever again.'

'Surely being a television mast can't be more important than being a scarecrow?' queried Statistic.

'Ah, now that's where you are wrong Statistic' answered Fedwink, 'I am not just a television mast, I am actually 'Head of Farm Entertainment.'

Or so Fedwink told everyone.

'I suppose being fixed to the top of the roof of the tallest barn on the farm is about as high a job as anyone can have' added Buxton the Blackbird chuckling loudly at his own little joke.

'Not bad for someone who was just a handle for a broom only four years ago, eh Statistic?' said Fedwink proudly.

That night Buxton, Bakewell and the rest of the birds crammed onto Fedwink's arms and squawked, chirped and laughed until, at nine o'clock, Statistic the Sparrow looked at his watch and told them it was about time they all went home to bed.

At that very moment from inside the farm house the Farmer's wife turned to her husband and said, 'I have just broken the handle of my kitchen broom.' 'Do you have any thing with which to fix it?' she added.

The Farmer glanced up at the roof of the old barn and pondered.

'Of course I do my dear, I know exactly where I can find just what you are looking for,' he replied. 'Ever since I erected the new aerials, television reception has been really poor anyway, it's just interference and whistling.'

Statistic only saw Fedwink once after that particular night. He was leaning against the kitchen door. During his lunch break of course.

It appeared that Fedwink had been asked if he would like to be in charge of 'internal cleaning and catering activities' in the farmhouse kitchen.

Probably the most important farm job of all.

Or so Fedwink told Statistic.

The end

7.

Goffle, the king and the twisted rainbow.

'I think we might have a teensy weensy problem your Majesty,' Fundle said to the King early one morning. 'It looks as though the north wind huffed and puffed so much last night it has managed to twist the rainbow.'

'Twist the rainbow???' the King shouted loudly, 'the north wind has twisted OUR famous rainbow? Where is the wind now, Fundle, we'll chop its head off.'

'I don't think the wind has a head to chop off your Majesty,' said Fundle.

'Well in that case we will put it in the dungeons for a year or so without any food.'

'It looks as though it has gone away Sir. As soon as it realised what it had done it stopped blowing and left… and very quickly by all accounts,' added Fundle. 'I have already told Cronk, Grog and Wedge to tie some ropes around either end to stop it twisting any further. They have already tried hitting it with a large hammer but they can't seem to twist it back into shape.'

'Hit it with a hammer! You can't hit our precious rainbow with a hammer you numbskull. It will crack and shatter into tiny pieces.'

'Then what do you suggest we do Sir? The annual rainbow contest is only one week away and we can't enter a rainbow that's twisted now can we,' said Fundle.

'Hmmm,' thought the King as he stroked and pulled at his long bushy beard. 'What about that Goffle fellow? Last summer he managed to make the moon glow dimmer at night because it was too bright and keeping me awake. I'm sure he could do it.'

'You never paid him for the last job your Majesty. He was hoping the money you promised would allow him to build a house for his poor wife and family,' Fundle replied.

'Well tell him if he doesn't do it we will, er, knock his house down.'

I don't think that would worry him too much Sir. I don't think he has been able to afford to build one yet,' replied Fundle.

'In that case we will chop his head off instead. I presume he has one of those Fundle?'

'Yes Sir, I believe he has.'

'Then get on with it Fundle! We only have one week before the contest starts and you know it takes a good two days just to clean and polish the rainbow. If we fail Fundle, you will be to blame, and you know what that means...'

It didn't take Fundle, Cronk, Grog and Wedge too long to find where Goffle was living and once they mentioned "The King", "Goffle's head" and the word "chop", he was more than willing to take on the job of removing the twist from the rainbow.

'Right Goffle, this is the deal,' said the King pointing his finger. 'You straighten the rainbow in readiness for the contest next week and I will give you enough money to build a new house for yourself and your poor family. If there is anything you need just talk to Fundle and you shall have it,' he added.

'But Sir,' said Goffle, 'you promised me the same thing when I dimmed the brightness from the moon for you last summer so you could sleep better at night.'

The King ignored Goffle's comment and whistled loudly as he continued sharpening and honing the edge of his axe on the grindstone.

Goffle sighed loudly and, rather reluctantly, began to think of ways to remove the twist from the rainbow.

'I think I have an idea that may work,' he said to himself.

First, he separated the rainbow into the seven visible colours using a very, very sharp knife and one by one he carefully took each of them down and laid them on the grassy meadow in front of the castle.

Then, with the use of a warm stone, some brown bread and a cup full of vinegar, he ironed each of them until they were perfectly flat before finally sewing them all back together again using multicoloured magical glass thread.

'I am going to need two large pots,' said Goffle to Fundle a few days later. 'I need to carefully place one under either end, just to make sure the rainbow doesn't twist itself back again. These need to be very heavy and I think they should be filled with gold.'

Fundle and Cronk, spent most of the day filling the pots with coins from the King's safe, whilst Grog and Wedge held on tightly to some ropes just as Goffle had instructed.

With just two days to go before the contest began the rainbow was back in place with no sign whatsoever of it ever having been twisted. Everyone in the town clapped and cheered and sang a little song about how Goffle had indeed completed a marvellous job.

'I will pay you as soon as the contest is over,' sniggered the King when Goffle finally went to the castle to collect his money.

Goffle sighed once again, turned and walked away.

The King's rainbow didn't win first prize on the day of the contest, nor did it win second or third for that matter. In fact the judges disqualified it because all the colours were upside down.

Goffle now lives with his wife and children in a land far, far away in the most beautiful house you could ever imagine.

To this very day no-one has ever found those two pots filled with gold that were carefully placed under either end of the rainbow...

The end

8.
The deep dark lake.

Whipsnade the duckling, Twink the donkey and Bristow the little pink pig lived in Farmer Turnip's old wooden barn, and they were the very best of friends. They would play together from the time Vince the rooster woke them in the morning until their mothers called them in for bed at night.

They were cheeky little youngsters and always up to some mischief or another.

Sitting on a perch high in the rafters of the same old barn lived Cromwell the wise old owl. From his perch Cromwell was able to see all the happenings in and around the farm and whenever Whipsnade, Twink and Bristow got into trouble he would hoot and hoot in disbelief and shake his head from side to side.

Sometimes, when they were really naughty, he would even fly down from his perch and give the three of them a good scolding. Then and only then would they stop being mischievous. But it never lasted all that long and by the time Cromwell had flown back to his perch they were up to something wicked yet again.

'Why don't we go down to the deep dark lake tomorrow and see if we can find Raggi Roo,' quacked Whipsnade, and Bristow and Twink thought it was a brilliantly great idea.

'We are not allowed,' brayed Twink, 'it's supposed to be dangerous down there.' 'So what would happen if someone should ever find out?' chuckled Bristow. 'Nothing at all,' they all shouted together and laughed out loud.

On the other side of the wood, just behind the farm, there was a small lake, the centre of which was supposed to be very, very deep and very, very dark.

There were rumours amongst the animals on the farm that a big ugly monster called Raggi Roo lived and lurked at the bottom of the deepest and darkest part of the lake and he would only come to the surface if he were ever hungry.

Not one of the animals on the farm ever went near there, just in case these rumours were true! And everyone knows what a monster can do.

Nevertheless, early the following morning, soon after breakfast, the three mischievous friends quietly left the farmyard, walked along the path down through the woods and stood at the side of the lake.

One by one they leaned over the rocky edge and looked down into the calm, deep, dark waters.

'**Arghhhhhhh.**'
It was Bristow who cried out first, and he turned and fled back towards the farmhouse as fast as his little trotters could carry him.

'**Arghhhhhh**'
Cried Whipsnade and Twink at just about the same time, and just as loudly, and they too ran back through the woods as if their lives depended on it.

'I saw Raggi Roo swimming in the water,' brayed Twink breathing heavily as he galloped back along the path through the woods.
'So did I,' quacked Whipsnade. 'Me too, me too,' grunted Bristow.

'What shall we do?' they said to each other when, out of breath, they finally reached the open gate that lead back into the safety of the farmyard. 'Don't you think we had better let Cromwell know what we have seen so that he can tell all the other animals that there really is a monster in the lake and to warn them not to go near there?' said Bristow.

The other two thought about it, argued and then, rather reluctantly, agreed.

'I don't think Cromwell is going to be very pleased with us though,' brayed Twink as the three friends wandered slowly across the farmyard towards the barn.

Cromwell the owl was sitting on his favourite perch when the three friends pushed open the old wooden door at the front of the barn.

'I get this feeling even before you speak that you three have been up to some no good or other yet again,' hooted Cromwell sternly.

'Well, not really,' quacked Whipsnade, 'it's just that we thought we had better tell you that we have all seen *Raggi Roo*.'

'*Raggi Roo*?' hooted Cromwell loudly. 'You three have actually seen the monster *Raggi Roo*?'

'So where exactly did you see this, *Raggi Roo*,' he added.

'Well we were playing quietly in the farmyard when…' Twink began to answer when the owl interrupted him.

'Don't tell me, I know, you three have been down to the deep dark lake,' Cromwell said staring closely at each one of them in turn. 'How many times have you been told that there is no monster called *Raggi Roo* lurking in the waters of the lake?'

'Yes there is, yes there is,' they all chimed together, 'we have seen him.' 'It was the most frightening face I have ever seen in my life,' quacked Whipsnade.

'And me too, really scary it was,' brayed Twink.
''Orrible, just 'orrible,' grunted Bristow. 'We all saw it, we all saw the monster swimming in the water,' he added and he squealed in fright at the top of his voice.

'So what did this monster, *Raggi Roo*, actually look like?' said Cromwell glancing once more at each of them in turn.

'He had a very, very large head and tall pointy ears,' brayed Twink, 'the biggest and ugliest ears I have ever seen in my life.'

'Hmmmm. Tell me young Twink,' said Cromwell, 'do you remember the story about Little Red Riding Hood and the Big Bad Wolf that your mother used to tell you when you were a little donkey?'

Twink nodded slowly.

'Then if there really is a monster with a head and ears that big then the easier it is for him to listen for the sound of your hooves and know exactly where you are if you are ever doing anything wrong.'

Twink gasped in horror and his ears flopped down over his eyes.

'And his nose was the largest and ugliest nose I have ever seen in my life,' grunted Bristow, 'and he was looking straight at me. 'Orrible piercing pink eyes they were, and so close together,' and Bristow started to shiver as he remembered what he had seen.

'Hmmm. Tell me Bristow,' said Cromwell, 'do you remember that very same story about Little Red Riding Hood and the Big Bad Wolf that your mother used to tell you when you were a little piglet?'

Bristow nodded slowly.

'Then if there really is a monster with a large nose and piercing eyes then all the easier it is for him to smell where you are and to see if you are doing anything wrong,' said Cromwell.

Bristow gasped in horror and his eyes opened wide.

'Well I think I had the biggest fright of all,' quacked Whipsnade, 'it was his mouth, it was bright orange in colour and when I looked down at him in the water it even started to open and it became bigger and bigger and bigger.' Whipsnade started to shiver in fright. 'In fact it opened so wide that I thought he was going to swallow me up. So I ran.'

'Hmmm. Tell me Whipsnade,' said Cromwell once again, 'do you also remember that very same story about Little Red Riding Hood and the Big Bad Wolf that your mother used to tell you when you were a duckling?'

Whipsnade nodded in agreement.

'Then if there really is a monster with a mouth that could open that wide then all the easier it would be for him to swallow you up whole if he caught you doing anything wrong,' added Cromwell.

Whipsnade gasped in horror at the thought of being caught and swallowed up.

'Now let us all think about this for a moment,' said Cromwell, and he pretended to rub his chin with his wing as though he were deep in thought.

'Twink saw a monster that had a large head and long pointy ears. Bristow saw a monster that had a big ugly nose and eyes that were bright pink and very close together. Whipsnade saw a monster that had an extremely wide orange mouth that opened wider than anything he had ever seen before in his life.

Until now I never believed that there was a monster called *Raggi Roo* living in the deep dark waters of the lake but you three have just convinced me that it must be true. In fact I am beginning to think that you may well have seen three *Raggi Roos* in the lake not just one. I think I would like to keep this a secret between the four of us. We don't want to frighten the other animals on the farm now do we, they are all so well behaved,' Cromwell whispered from behind his wing.

Whipsnade, Bristow and Twink agreed not to say anything to anyone and even told Cromwell that from now on they would never be naughty again and they would never ever visit the lake or look down into the deep dark waters in search of *Raggi Roo*.

They became three of the best-behaved youngsters on the farm.

Well, for a short while anyway.

Back at the lake, the usually calm surface of the water started to ripple violently and suddenly a rather large head broke the surface. It had long pointy ears, an ugly nose with a wide orange mouth and piercing pink eyes that were very, very close together.

It slowly looked all around, took a long deep breath before disappearing back down into the waters of the deep, dark lake.

The end

9.

As if by magic.

'Can you please keep quiet,' clucked Piff the little red speckled hen, 'How on earth am I supposed to concentrate with all that noise going on?'

'Well what are you actually doing that needs so much concentration?' replied Conroy the noisiest and loudest cockerel who lived on the same farm as little Piff.

'I can't tell you because it's a er, it's er secret,' whispered Piff holding up her right wing to shield her beak so none of the other chickens in the yard would hear.

'A secret! A secret!' squawked Conroy so loudly, every other chicken in the henhouse heard.

'Piff has got a secret, Piff has got a secret!' Conroy chanted at the top of his voice, whilst hopping from one foot to the other. All the other chickens in the coop suddenly stopped pecking, scratching, laying and whatever else they were doing and gathered around Conroy. They clucked and clacked in excitement so loudly that Piff began to wish she had never mentioned the word "secret" or said anything to Conroy at all.

Piff groaned and shook her little head from side to side.

'So what's this big secret Piff?' shouted Miffin one of the elder chickens that was standing at the back of the gathered flock.

'I was just trying to see if I could hear the grass grow,' clucked little Piff very quietly and rather pathetically.

'Did I hear you correctly,' said Miffin, 'you are trying to see if you can hear the grass grow?'

There was a deadly silence.

Neither one single cluck nor one single clack was heard from any of the hens in the yard. The chickens looked at each other for a few minutes and then burst into the loudest squawking and laughter you have ever heard in your life.

'Little Piff is listening to see if she can hear the grass growing!' squawked Miffin, and she instantly fell over onto her back and rolled from side to side, making so much noise all the other chickens fell over laughing as well, partly because of Piff and partly as a result of seeing Miffin rolling about in the yard.

'So why are you listening in the hope of hearing the grass grow Little Piff?' clucked Conroy, doing his very best not to join in with the rollicking laughter from the other chickens.

'Well, you see, the other morning whilst I was having breakfast I asked my Mum to tell me when I would be old enough to fly just like the blackbirds, crows and sparrows who live in those tall trees on the other side of the farmer's field. She told me as soon as I hear the grass growing beneath my feet, then, and only then will I be ready to fly.'

'But Piff, we are chickens and chickens can't really fly, and I don't think you will ever hear the grass growing either,' replied Conroy.

Piff was very disappointed indeed. Little tears trickled from her eyes, down over her beak and made small plopping sounds as they landed on the ground. She sobbed quietly to herself as she walked slowly back to her Mum who was sitting on their nest in the henhouse.

All the other chickens joked and laughed at her as she walked by.

'Piff thought she might hear the grass grow,' they all clucked and laughed, the way that chickens tend to do when they hear a really good joke about grass and hearing it grow.

'One of these days!' Piff said to herself, 'one of these days I will show them I'm right.'

It was just before breakfast the following morning when Conroy rushed into the henhouse and woke all the other chickens. He told them that Little Piff was standing on top of the highest roof of the tallest building in the farmyard and was about to jump off to prove to everyone she really could fly.

Every chicken and cockerel in the farm rushed into the yard and started calling out her name.

'We must stop her before she hurts herself,' clucked Conroy, 'the roof of the farmhouse is a very, very long way up indeed.'

'Please Piff, please don't try to fly, please come down off the roof. You are a chicken and chickens can't really fly,' they all shouted together.

'I can fly, I know I can fly,' replied Piff. 'You see, I was walking in the field early this morning before any of you were awake. It was really, really quiet and all of a sudden I heard the grass growing beneath my feet. That means I am old enough and ready to fly.'

The other chickens squawked as loud as they could to try their very best to stop Piff from plunging off the farmhouse roof, but it was all in vain.

Piff took one long deep breath, opened her tiny wings as wide as they would go and tumbled beak first towards the ground falling faster and faster with every second. The chickens in the yard gasped in horror, screamed and shouted and hugged each other in fright.

Then, at the very last moment, as if by magic, when Piff was just ten centimetres off the ground she swooped to the left and soared upwards over the roof of the old henhouse, above the barn and high into the cloudless, blue sky.

There were squawks of disbelief from below. Conroy, Miffin and the rest of the brood stood watching in total amazement as Piff twisted and turned, dived and soared.

'Well done Little Piff, well done. I said you could do it,' a rather high-pitched voice called out and instantly all the chickens stopped clucking and squawking and glanced across at each other.

'Who said that?' bellowed Conroy loudly, as he too looked all around. 'Now that's a bit scary,' clucked Miffin looking downwards, 'if I didn't know any better I would have said it was the grass that's growing beneath my feet!'

The end

10.
'It's all about to come to an end!'

'I must tell the King,' cried Sputnik the cheeky little monkey, scurrying through the trees with a very worried look on his face. 'This is terrible, terrible news, I just hope he will know exactly what to do.'

'What on earth is*sssssss* the matter *Sss*sputnik?' hissed Pertwee the puff adder who was standing guard in front of the King's Palace, 'why are you looking *sssssso* worried and shouting *ssssssso* loudly?'

'It's all about to come to an end Pertwee,' cried Sputnik, 'mark my words... I must let the King know,' and he hurried through the front gate and into the Palace where Drypuss the lion, King of the jungle, lived.

The King was in his sitting room enjoying his favourite tea, cheese and biscuits washed down with lashings of ginger beer.

'Your Majesty,' said Sputnik bowing slightly, 'please excuse me for interrupting your tea, but something terrible, terrible has happened and I fear it is about to get worse.'

'Now calm down Sputnik,' said the King, 'and tell me what the problem is and why you are so worried.'

'It's, it's, it's the moon your Majesty. I think someone has started to...to eat it.'

'Eat the moon?' gasped the King and half a cheesy biscuit fell out of his mouth and onto the palace floor. 'I can't believe it! Someone is eating the moon? Our moon? The jungle's moon?'

'It seems a rather strange thing for someone to eat, Sputnik. Do you have any idea who it could be, and, perhaps more importantly, why on earth they would want to eat it?'

'I most certainly do have evidence for you sir, but I am afraid I have not seen who ever is eating it' replied Sputnik, and he told the King the story about the moon.

He explained how just a few days ago he had looked up into the

55

night sky and the moon was a lovely big creamy yellow coloured ball. It was so bright; the light from it cascaded onto every tree, stone and bush growing in the jungle.

The following night, he told the King, there appeared to be just a teensy weensy bit of it missing. The King frowned, growled deeply, and leaned a little closer as Sputnik continued with his story. The next night, he added, there was a little bit more missing and the following night even more again.

'I think unless we can find out who is eating it sir, in a few more days it may be completely gone and the jungle will be plunged into darkness for ever more.'

'Well that certainly is a very interesting story young Sputnik,' said the King as he ran his sharp claws through his long brown mane. 'Perhaps you should stay here tonight. We will take a long look at it and see what happens and then decide what can be done.'

So, the King, Pertwee the guard and Sputnik stood side by side looking out of the palace window up into the night sky.

As they searched the heavens waiting for the moon to appear the King continued to munch slowly on his cheese and biscuits.

The little monkey stared at them longingly, wishing the King would at least offer him a piece of cheese. Just to taste.

Ever since Sputnik was a tiny little monkey he had always wanted to taste a piece of cheese, but never ever had the chance.

So, the three of them stared up into the sky as the sun went down and it slowly became dark.

It was almost half past quarter to from when the moon suddenly began to appear. Just as Sputnik had predicted, there was a rather large piece missing from one side of it.

'Oh my!' exclaimed Sputnik, 'there's even less of it tonight than there was last night Sir.'

The King gasped in surprise. Sputnik could well be right.

There was without doubt a rather large portion of the moon missing. It wasn't a big yellow round ball anymore.

The King nodded his head and had to agree, it most certainly did look as though someone was eating the moon.

'Well, why are they eating it?' questioned the King.

'Well,' said Sputnik, 'to become King of the jungle you obviously need to be a well educated lion, Sir. So, as you well know the moon is actually made of cheese.'

'Ah! Well! Yes! Of course, I, I, I, knew that Sputnik,' answered King Drypuss.

'Well I think it could be someone who likes eating cheese, your Majesty.'

'Well I like eating cheese, Sputnik, but it certainly wasn't me!' exclaimed the King pushing the plate that held the remains of the cheese and biscuits across the table as though he didn't care for them anymore.

'A mouse!' exclaimed the King, 'of course, it must be a mouse. They are always after my cheese.'

So he ordered Pertwee the guard to bring Sydmouth the mouse to the palace so he could have a "quiet word" with him, in private.

'I am an awfully small animal your Majesty,' squeaked Sydmouth on his arrival at the palace, and the moon is extremely large and very high in the sky. Even though I do like cheese I would never be able to reach it let alone eat it. You really should be looking for someone with a mouth that's much, much larger than mine.'

'A hippopotamus!' exclaimed the King, 'of course, it must be Hepworth the hippopotamus. He has the largest mouth in the whole jungle.'

So the King ordered Pertwee, the guard, to bring Hepworth to the palace so he could have a "quiet word" with him, in private.

'I must admit your Majesty,' bellowed Hepworth on his arrival at the palace, 'I do have a very large mouth, and a rather smelly one too I might add,' and he held his hoof up in front of his face as he burped rather long and very loudly. 'But even though I quite like cheese I am still too short, and much too fat to jump. I just cannot reach the moon. You really should be looking for someone a lot taller than me.'

'A giraffe!' exclaimed the King 'of course it must be Lonsdale the giraffe. He is certainly the tallest animal in the jungle.

So he ordered Pertwee, the guard, to bring Lonsdale to the palace so he could have a "quiet word" with him too, in private of course.

'Well, I do have quite a large mouth,' answered Lonsdale on his arrival at the palace, 'and giraffes are the tallest animals in the jungle. I could probably reach the moon if I stretched high enough on my back legs, and on tiptoe, and poked my long tongue out as far as it could go. But the truth of the matter is, your Majesty, I simply do not like cheese. You see we giraffes are highleafetarians. We only eat leaves, and even then only those growing on the very tops of the trees.'

'I fear all may be lost Sputnik,' said the King munching on yet another piece of cheese and biscuit. 'I don't think we are ever going to find out who has been eating our moon. It's sad to say that in just a few days time the jungle could be in complete darkness.'

'One moment, Sir, I have just had a most brilliantly good idea,' said the monkey.

'If you were to give me enough cheese I could probably repair the moon and stop it from disappearing.'

The King thought about Sputnik's proposal and in no time at all proclaimed the idea as "first class" and ordered him to set about collecting cheese to repair the moon.

'To be started immediately,' the King proclaimed.

Sputnik told everyone he would need lots of Cheddar cheese, because pale yellow was the main colour of the moon.

He would also need some Red Leicester cheese for those really bright summer nights.

He also needed some Gorgonzola cheese as well, because the moon had a few spotty blue bits in certain places.

By the time Sputnik had collected all the cheese he needed to repair the moon there was nothing left for King Drypuss to eat with his biscuits at teatime.

Each night the King, in despair, looked out of the window of his palace and up into the sky as the moon became smaller and smaller.

Then, on the night after it had almost disappeared from view, to the King's delight, it slowly began to grow larger and larger again in the clear night sky.

The King was full of joy that Sputnik's idea had been a success and their moon would once again cascade light over the animals, trees and bushes in the jungle.

He secretly wished, however, he could take a bite out of it himself, as he hadn't tasted any cheese for a long, long time.

King Drypuss did think it rather annoying, however, that as soon as Sputnik finished repairing the moon someone, almost immediately, started to eat it again.

So Sputnik needed to collect more cheese in readiness for the next repair.

'I am really missing my cheese and biscuits at tea time,' said the King to his guard one evening. 'Biscuits and biscuits just aren't quite the same.'

'Sputnik, the little monkey is doing a super job repairing the moon though, don't you think Pertwee?'

'Yessssssssir,' replied the puff adder, 'but he's not ssssssssuch a "little" monkey now.

He *sssssss*eems to have put on quite a bit of weight over the last few months.'

'Hmmmmm!' pondered the King, and as he thought about Pertwee's reply his big black eyes narrowed into two fine and fearsome slits.

'Hmmmmm?' queried the puff adder.

'Bring the cheeky little monkey to the palace Pertwee, I think I would like a quiet word with him, in private.'

'And Pertwee?'

'Ye*sssssss* your Majesty.'

'I think it could be cheese and biscuits for tea again tonight.'

'Would that be for one, or two your Maje*sssssssss*ty?'

'Just for one Pertwee, just for one.

I think for *a certain* cheeky little monkey it's all about to come to an end.'

The end

11.

Delworth and Woppit's day at the seaside.

Delworth and Woppit were the very best of friends.

They had known each other since they were tiny grubs and had grown up together on the farm they now called home.

They went to school together, they played together, and they both enjoyed exactly the same things. Buzzing noisily up and down a pane of glass was one of their favourite. Flying about pretending they didn't know where they were going was another. But their best game of all was landing on the farmer's dinner and when he wasn't looking, being sick on it.

Delworth and Woppit were two dung flies and they really enjoyed their life on the farm. They could not wait to get up in the morning and set off for what the two of them considered to be work.

There were always fresh cowpats in the fields for them both to settle on and they both loved the fresh smell of dung more than anything else in the whole wide world. They would buzz and wiz from one cowpat to another all day long and the fresher the cowpat the better.

'Oh, this is the life!' Delworth would smile and say to Woppit as their little feet patted and puddled on the soft surface of the smelly poo.

'Fresh air and the whole countryside to fly around in, brilliant!' Woppit would add.

'In fact, "Oh to be a Dung Fly" hey, Del?' chuckled Woppit rather intellectually as he nudged his friend with one of his wings. The words, as Delworth knew, came from the title of a very important 'Dung Fly' poem they had both read and enjoyed whilst studying for a literature exam in their first year of junior school.

'I've been thinking,' uttered Delworth one particular morning, 'we work every day without really stopping for breakfast, lunch or even tea. We work up to eighteen hours a day in the summer, and seven days a week without taking a single day off. I think we deserve a proper holiday.'

'Whoo, hoo Del, an excellent idea,' replied Woppit. 'I'm all for holidays.'

'What about visiting our friends and relatives on the farm just up the lane?' he added rather excitedly. We haven't been up there since the apples fell off the trees a year last autumn.'

'Hmmmm,' exclaimed Delworth sensing his best friend's apparent lack of interest in doing something completely different and exciting just for once.

'I suppose you'll be wanting to fly over and see the exhibits in the National Dung Museum next?' replied Delworth.

Before Woppit had chance to open his mouth and reply, Delworth said 'No, I mean a real holiday, just for a change. Somewhere warm, exciting and different. Somewhere we can meet different flies and talk about football. Perhaps tasting different foods and cuisines even.'

'Sipping cola from someone else's glass?' added Woppit and a cheeky smile appeared on his face.

'I was thinking more about a day at the… the seaside actually,' said Delworth, 'we have never ever been there,' and he winked at Woppit with the rather large eye on the right-hand side of his head.

'Crazy, crazy idea indeed Del baby!' answered Woppit, 'wheeee, count me in good buddy,' and he buzzed and flitted back and forth across the corner of the field, where they had been working all morning.

'Lets go tomorrow Del,' Woppit added rather excitedly.

'We can finish off here tonight, pack a few things, and leave first thing in the morning before the skies get too busy with bees and wasps.'

The two friends became really excited about the prospect of going on holiday and made a few notes of things they wanted to take with them for the day.

'I would like to take a football,' buzzed Woppit rather loudly before settling back down on a rather squidgy apple stump.

'Then I shall take my Frisbee,' added Delworth, smiling.

'Oh, and a bucket and spade so we can dig in the sand,' they both said together and buzzed out loud.

Delworth and Woppit didn't get a lot of sleep that night as they carefully planned their trip to the seaside the following day.

'Do you know which way it is to the seaside Del?' said Woppit as he finished packing his bag.

'Er, that way I think,' replied Delworth not really pointing in any direction at all.

'That's sure good enough for me lil' buddy,' replied Woppit and they both closed their eyes and finally fell fast asleep.

The next morning, even before the first birds started tuning up in readiness for the dawn chorus and well before the sun began to peek over the hedge and into the meadows, the two friends had finished their breakfasts, packed their rucksacks and were ready to set off for the seaside.

'This is the life Woppit,' commented Delworth, 'we're both going on a summer holiday,' and he started to hum the tune of an old Cliff Richard song whilst Woppit, who was a big Cliff Richard and Elvis fan, even sang the words.

It wasn't all that long before the two friends were perched side by side on top of a candyfloss van that stood in the middle of the promenade overlooking a golden sandy beach and a deep blue sea.

'Wow!' uttered Woppit.

'Wow indeed!' replied Delworth.

'I never ever thought it would be like this,' he added.

'Nothing like I expected either,' exclaimed Woppit.

'Look Del there's a few houseflies over by those rocks, and a couple of bluebottles and greenbottles near that washed up piece of seaweed. Oh! And there's a family of sand flies sitting on an old chocolate wrapper under the wastepaper bin.'

'But, just look at the rest of it little buddy. It's…disgusting.

It's absolutely covered in smelly, noisy, horrible human beings. They are either making a nuisance of themselves by running around needlessly or shouting at the tops of their voices.

In fact there is hardly any room left on the beach for us to play.'

The two friends buzzed back and forth across the sand looking for somewhere nice and quiet to stop, but there were very few empty spaces.

When the two friends finally found a nice warm towel on which to sit, some nasty little child, wearing a white cotton hat with "I love my Mum" printed on it, started kicking sand in their faces. He even tried to hit them with a spade.

'Look out Del!' yelled Woppit when he saw the child raise the spade above his head.

'Yipes, that was close,' said Delworth as he only just managed to dodge the spade as it thwacked into the towel where, not a second ago, Delworth had been sitting.

'Not sure I like the seaside after all,' he added. 'It's rather dangerous, perhaps we should go back home, it's a lot safer there, and far less crowded.'

And so the two friends, rather disappointedly, set off back towards the farm without kicking Woppit's football, without playing with Delworth's Frisbee, or without playing in the soft golden sand with their buckets and spades.

In fact, they hadn't even taken their rucksacks off their backs.

Early the following morning back in the farmer's field, just as the birds began to wake and the sun began to cast its warm shadowy glow across the meadows, the two friends stood together on a nice warm fresh cowpat.

'Just take a deep breath Woppit and tell me what you can smell.'

Woppit breathed in deeply as he was asked then slowly breathed back out.

'*Ahhhhhh!*' he buzzed and he closed his eyes in delight.

'Home sweet home, Del, home sweet home!'

The end

12.

The sportsman.

Gloop the giraffe, Gengis the cheetah and Spon the hippopotamus were relaxing in the shade of the Yucapoola trees on the bank of the Zimboo River, discussing Saturday's sport, as they always did on Sunday afternoons.

'Did I ever tell you I used to be a world class runner?' purred Gengis as he raised his head in the air rather smugly. 'I even competed in the "Jungle Games" some five years ago. The sixty metres chase was my best event and I came second in the final. I was pipped to the post by one of those gazelle creatures. I just could not catch him. That's how I got my nickname you see. Swifty – the fastest animal on two, er three, I mean four legs.'

'So that makes you the fastest animal in the jungle except for the gazelle that managed to beat you,' sniggered Thimble the hyena, who was sitting a little higher up on the riverbank, overlooking the three friends.

Thimble disliked sport more than anything else in the whole wide world. He couldn't really see the point of it all. Running, jumping, bat and ball... In fact the only things Thimble enjoyed doing were reading comic books and watching silly comedy shows, especially the ones showing late on a Sunday evening.

'Well anyway, I was nearly jungle champion once,' added Gengis and he turned, bared his teeth and hissed at Thimble.

'Did I ever tell you I used to play for a football team?' Gloop the giraffe added rather proudly.

'I was a striker.

I played up front.

Always hungry for goals, me.

I had a number nine on the back of my shirt.

Two years ago we were in the cup final and I was picked to play because I was better at heading the ball than anyone else in the team. That's why they nicknamed me Noddy.'

'Did your team win the cup Gloop?' enquired Gengis.

'Well, we didn't quite win it but we were a very close second,' he replied.

'So you were second out of two,' Thimble added, rolling about in laughter. 'That means, now let me see, ah yes, you ended up beaten and came last?'

'Did you score any goals Gloop?' Spon asked, trying hard to ignore Thimble's comments.

'Well, not really. I did have a number of high crosses to head but they all missed the net.'

'Well no wonder they didn't go in the goal you long-necked dozy bib, you are fifteen feet tall and the goals are just eight feet high. You probably headed every ball seven feet over the crossbar!' and with that Thimble collapsed onto his back in laughter almost rolling down the bank and into the river.

'I was always good at snooker!' bellowed Spon in a deep gruff voice following a few minutes of silence. 'In fact I still have my cue,' he added and proudly showed everyone a rather long tree branch that had all its leaves whittled off. 'I nearly won the championship with this three years ago!'

The other two gazed in awe and wonder as Spon held his prize wooden twig high in the air for all to see.

'Wow!' they both said together.

'So that's the actual bat you used is it Spon?' added Gengis, looking amazed.

'A snookerist? Spon the hippopotamus was a snookerist?' Thimble repeated, sniggering loudly and trying hard to control his laughter.

'Yes, I remember it as though it were yesterday,' said Spon. 'It was the last game of the tournament, sixty points each, and the only ball left on the table was the black.'

'So where was the little white ball then?' interrupted Thimble, and once again he burst into yet another bout of high-pitched hysterical laughter.

Spon ignored the comment and continued with his story whilst holding his cue and pretending to line up for a shot.

'It was an easy pot, black into the bottom right hand pocket. I just needed to rest one of my back legs on the table so I could comfortably play the ball.'

'Well... what happened next?' enquired Gloop after a rather long pause. 'Did you pot it?'

'Hmmmm, not really,' answered Spon.

'So you missed it then?' added Gengis rather disappointedly.

'Hmmm, well yes and sort of no' bellowed Spon. 'You see, as I leaned on the table to play the shot the legs sort of collapsed under my weight and it broke in half. The white ball rolled all the way down the table and dropped into the pocket first. So the referee awarded the match to Bartrum the chimpanzee.

All the animals who came to watch the game burst out laughing, it was so embarrassing.'

'So that's how you got the nickname Beetroot!' said Thimble and he erupted into hysterical laughter yet again.

Spon blushed rather shyly and nodded in agreement.

'I think it's time I set off for home,' Thimble said to himself and left. 'Nicknames! It's all too much for me. Why is it always sportsmen who seem to have the most ridiculous nicknames? What did the other animals call me at one time? Ah yes; now I remember, "Bogey". Now that's a proper nickname. They never told me why they called me

Bogey though?' Thimble said to himself rather quizzically and immediately started picking his nose.

That night, well after the evening sun had set below the tops of the Yucapoola trees, the echoes of a certain hyena's high-pitched hysterical laughter could still be heard for miles.

On this particular Sunday, for some, the evening comedy show had started rather early.

The end

13.

It all seems rather pointless.

'What have you found that's so funny to make you laugh so loudly, Gilbert?' said Finlay.

'You only have to look at them, I think they are so cute, and when I watch them it makes me feel well, sort of relaxed I suppose,' smiled Gilbert as he gazed through the sides of the large glass bowl.

'Hmmm, I think they are rather simple creatures,' added Finlay. 'All day long they just go around and around and around in their own little world for what appears to be no reason whatsoever. It all seems rather pointless to me. What are they supposed to be looking for? I bet they don't even know themselves.'

'I have noticed of late that whatever everyone else is doing it all seems to be rather pointless to you Finlay,' replied Gilbert.

'Look, look, look, watch this, one of them has found some food and all the others will suddenly appear as if from nowhere and begin to eat it. How do they do that? How do they know there is food? Who actually puts the food in there? I love watching them eat. They always seem willing to share everything with each other and enjoy it at the same time. Sometimes, when they are eating their mouths are open so wide you could almost think they were talking to each other.'

'What? Do you really think they talk to each other, just like us Gilbert?' said Finlay suddenly looking that little bit closer through the glass and with a little more interest.

'Hmmmm,' said Gilbert and he stopped for a moment to think. 'Well now you come to mention it, do you know, I've never thought about that before. Perhaps they are talking to each other whilst they are eating. Mind you, I have never heard them say anything, have you?' Gilbert added.

'Nnnnnnnope, I don't think so anyway,' said Finlay, trying desperately hard to look as though he was actually interested in what his friend was saying.

'In some ways I feel really sorry for them,' said Gilbert, 'as I have heard it said that they find it difficult to remember things.'

'Cripes, that must be awful not being able to remember things. Perhaps it's just because there is nothing of importance in their lives that needs to be remembered,' added Finlay rather philosophically.

'After all, what is the point in trying to remember pointless things?'

Gilbert thought carefully about Finlay's last comment and then nodded his head slowly in agreement.

'What I find most exciting is when they come really close to the glass and stare through it as though they are watching us to see what we are doing,' said Gilbert and he started to chuckle loudly, and Finlay joined in.

'What have you found that's so funny that has made us both laugh so loudly Gilbert?' said Finlay.

'Eh?' Replied Gilbert.

'Didn't you ask me that very same question just a few moments ago?' he added.

'Nnnnnno, I don't think so; it must have been someone else. I think I have always had a very good memory for things like that. In fact I am sure that if I had asked you that question before I would definitely have remembered. Anyway I've been swimming around near that large shell on the other side of the bowl for most of the afternoon, I think. It's been a rather pointless day really.'

'Just as I thought, it was you who asked the question,' uttered Gilbert. 'I've suddenly remembered, there is no "someone else" it just so happens there's only two of us actually swimming in this bowl.'

'Was me what?' replied Finlay as he franticly began to forage in the stones and gravel that were lying on the bottom of the bowl.

'Have you found anything?' asked Gilbert a few moments later.

'Errrrrrrrr no, not really,' replied Finlay, 'in fact now you have come to mention it, I think I might have forgotten what I am supposed to be looking for!'

'Ah, so maybe you are correct after all, perhaps life is rather pointless, for some of us,' concluded Gilbert, and his tail swished back and forth as he made his way slowly up through the water to the top of the bowl.

'Pardon me?' said Finlay, looking quite hurt.

'Sorry, I can't repeat it as I can't remember what I just said, ' replied Gilbert, and as he continued on upwards a smile began to appear on his face.

'Hmmm,' Finlay muttered to himself as he continued on his search through the stones and gravel, looking for something special but he couldn't quite remember what the something special was.

'Rather pointless eh!' he chuckled, 'he'll soon change his mind if ever I find whatever it is I am supposed to be looking for in this gravel.'

The end

14.

Whimaway's dilemma.

'Ooooh, oooh, oooh' whimpered Whimaway the baby Elephant as he scurried home from his first day at school, with a rucksack on his back that was full of brand new books.

'Miss Chizlewick, our teacher, was telling us that every animal in the whole wide world knows elephants are really clever and have the bestest memories of all. She said we never ever forget anything we have remembered,' he told his mother.

'Mmmmmm!' replied his Mum rather quizzically, 'teachers are usually right.'

'Well, I am a little worried that I can't be a very clever elephant, Mum, because I really think I may well have forgotten something' added Whimaway shaking his little trunk back and forth.

'Now, are you sure you think you have forgotten something Whimaway?' said his mother, who at the time was rather more concerned with making herself a nice cup of strong tea than she was about listening to her son's silly schoolboy chatter.

'After all, today was only your first day at school so perhaps there was nothing for you to remember in the first place?' she added.

'There was loads and loads of things for us to remember Mum,' he replied rather worriedly.

'In fact I don't think there is enough room left in my memory for me to remember any more unless I start to forget some of those I have already remembered. The good thing is if I did, I will then have enough room to remember more new things. But there are lots of things I remember that I don't want to forget and I could accidentally forget something important that I really, really want to remember. What ever shall I do Mum?' he added with a whimper and a few tears slipped from his sad brown eyes, down his trunk and sploshed onto the kitchen floor.

Whimaway's Mum looked slightly confused by it all and took one long sip out of her teacup as she gave the problem some thought.

'Your father will be home in ten minutes, you can tell him exactly what you have told me and he can answer your question. He is far better at answering technical questions than I am,' she replied.

Now, elephants, as well as having the best memories of all animals, are also well known for their excellent timekeeping. Precisely ten minutes later, not one second early nor one second late, Whimaway's father arrived home from work and Whimaway told him exactly what he had, only ten minutes earlier, told his mother.

'Well if you have already told your mother and you have remembered to tell me then you must still have room in your memory to remember,' his father replied with a clever looking smirky smile on his face.

The sort of clever smirky smile that a father always seems to have. Whimaway's mother nodded in agreement.

'That is unless there is something you have might have accidentally forgotten, I suppose,' his father added, throwing, once again, that little bit of confusion into the conversation.

'Ooooh!' said Whimaway a little sad and dejected.

'Well, how will I know if I have accidentally forgotten something Dad?'

'That's a very good question indeed son,' his father replied, 'and the simple answer is what ever you have forgotten you will never remember it again so it probably will not matter.'

'Yes but what will matter is if I have forgotten something I really wanted to remember and now I can't remember it,' Whimaway replied.

'Perhaps if I knew what I had forgotten I may be able to re-remember it,' he added excitedly and a big beaming smile appeared on Whimaway's face.

'Have you ever had to re-remember anything? Dad. Is it an easy thing to do?'

'Well yes, er, I mean no Whimaway, I haven't. Surely if you could remember what you have forgotten then you haven't really forgotten it so there would be no reason to re-remember it.'

'But what if in the meantime I had re-forgotten it as well?'
added Whimaway.

There was a few minutes silence as Whimaway's father gave the
question some thought before he answered.

'You can't re-forget something Whimaway' his father replied raising
his voice quite considerably as he lowered his newspaper and gazed
across the room at the little elephant. 'If you have forgotten it then
you have forgotten it.'

'But elephants are never supposed to forget Dad!'

'So,' Whimaway trumpeted loudly, 'have you ever forgotten anything?'

'Your mother and I have never ever forgotten anything in all our
lives, bellowed the older elephant loudly, 'and I am sure your mother
will agree with that.'

Whimaway's mother's head appeared at the door and she nodded
in agreement.

'In that case how old do you think you were when you first
remembered you had to remember everything?' asked Whimaway.

'Oh! I don't know, perhaps one or two or even twelve, I can't
remember that it was a long, long time ago.'

'Oooooh' exclaimed Whimaway and he raised his little trunk high into
the air and trumpeted rather cheekily.

Whimaway's father glared over the top of his reading glasses, rolled
his newspaper into what appeared to look like a rather long and thick
stick and raised it slowly above his head.

'Tea is ready' trumpeted Whimaway's Mum from the kitchen, much
to Whimaway's relief and the family gathered around the table to eat.

'I do believe you have forgotten to put tomato ketchup on my chips mother,' said Whimaway's father as he began to tuck into his meal.

'Oooooh' exclaimed Whimaway, and he raised his little trunk high in the air and trumpeted a little louder than he did before.

So, it's not really true what our teacher, Miss Chizlewick said, it seems to me that even elephants can forget.'

The end

15.
The dreamers.

'Da-ad,' said Chelford early one morning as they both sat at the kitchen table eating breakfast.

'Mickey Drippin, in 1B, told me he has a really exciting dream nearly every night when he goes to bed. The other night he told me he dreamt he played a great game of football and scored four goals, and against Arsenal as well.

Why is it, Da-ad, I never dream? I really wish I was clever enough to dream an exciting dream like the ones Mickey has.'

'Do you dream Daaaad, cos you are always telling me you are really, really clever.'

'Well, let me think,' his father replied whilst rubbing his chin.

'Yes, son you do need to be clever but you don't have to be really clever to dream. You see, lots of people are clever enough to dream, Chelford, but the really, really clever ones are those who catch their dreams and remember them. But just one thing Chelford, there is always the dimwit who cannot tell the difference between a dream and reality,' and Chelford's father chuckled quietly as he left for work.

'Hmmmm,' pondered Chelford, 'so to start with I need to be clever to dream but I need to be really clever to catch the dream so I will remember it in the morning. That sounds easy enough.'

A big beaming smile began to appear on Chelford's face as he thought long and hard about his father's advice.

That afternoon, as soon as Chelford arrived home from school, he began searching through his father's shed for something he could use to catch a dream.

In a large chest he found some old wooden mousetraps and wondered if they might come in handy just in case he needed to catch any small dreams.

On the top shelf he found his old baseball pitcher's glove. That, Chelford thought, would be ideal for catching any medium-size dream.

'Now what if I ever have a long dream that needs to be caught?' he said to himself. He looked in the sports cupboard where he knew he would find a bat and ball and an old net he and his brother used just last summer on their table tennis table.

'Yes! Ideal for even the longest of dreams,' said Chelford proudly.

Chelford carried the traps, the glove and the net upstairs to his room and carefully placed them on the floor near his bed. They were within easy reach should he need them in a hurry at any time during the night.

At 9 o'clock he turned off the bedroom light and quickly fell fast asleep.

'Da-ad,' said Chelford the very next morning as they were seated at the kitchen table eating breakfast. 'If I were to find something I could use to catch a small dream, a medium size dream and also a long dream and then I still can't remember them, does it mean I am not clever enough to dream or am I just not very good at catching them?'

'Well, let me see,' his father replied, 'you are five after all and almost grown up. Now even though you may well have caught the dream, unless you had something to keep it in until the following morning when you wake up, it has probably escaped and will be lost forever. Dreams can be very wriggly, tricky things sometimes Chelford,' his father added, and winked.

That afternoon as soon as Chelford returned home from school he began searching through all the drawers in the house, the cupboards in the garage and even on the shelves in the attic, looking for tins, cardboard and plastic boxes, bottles with corks and jars with lids. In fact anything he could take up to his bedroom and into which he could store all different kinds of dreams ready for the following morning.

At 9 o'clock that night Chelford turned off his bedroom light and quickly fell fast asleep.

It was early the following morning when Chelford's father walked past Chelford's open bedroom door. He noticed that along one side of the room there were boxes, tins, bottles and jars all carefully stacked and clearly marked with sticky white labels. Some even had writing on them.

Intrigued by what Chelford had been doing, his father took a closer look and saw the label on one biscuit box read: **'Chelford Helps Doctor Who Escape from the Forbidden Planet.'**

On the label of one of the screw-topped pickle onion jars was written: **'Chelford Scores the Winning Goal against Charlton Athletic in the Cup Final.'**

'Very strange indeed!' he thought, and started pulling a cork out from a small brown bottle with a label on the side that read: **'Chelford Sets a New World Record for the Highest Ever Bungee Jump.'**

The instant the cork popped out, Chelford's father found himself high up in the sky and then hurtling head first towards the ground at terrific speed with just a thin elastic rope attached to his ankles.

As he sped downwards in total disbelief his eyes opened wider and wider and even wider still when he noticed beneath him the cold wet waters of a deep large lake. The elastic rope was stretched to its limit when Chelford's father's head, with a very loud "PLOP", sank deep into the cold wet water.

Not only had the water stopped him screaming, it had stopped him falling as well. Then, less than a second later, he was violently yanked back out, spitting and spluttering, and sent flying back up into the blue sky, the way bungee ropes tend to do once they have been stretched as far as they can go and can't go any further.

'Wow,' said Chelford's father when it was all over, 'that really was frightening.'

He continued reading the labels on the boxes and tins, for a few moments longer, before leaving Chelford's room and continuing across the landing down the stairs and into the kitchen.

'Da-ad,' said Chelford whilst they were seated at the kitchen table eating breakfast. 'I dreamt last night I had managed to capture all my dreams using traps, gloves and nets and I kept them all in boxes, tins and jars in my bedroom. I then made loads of pocket money selling them to my friends at school. Mickey Drippin bought three and told everyone they were the most exciting three dreams he had ever had in his life.'

'Well that's good news indeed Chelford, I did say you could be clever enough to dream and all you needed was that little something special to capture them for when you wake up the following morning.'

Chelford was indeed very pleased. It did seem that he was at last clever enough to dream and a big beaming smile appeared on his face as he watched his father drink his morning cup of tea.

'Da-ad, why is your hair wet?' said Chelford smiling as water dripped off his father's nose and onto the tablecloth.

'I don't really know,' his father replied, 'when I looked in the bathroom mirror this morning my hair, my face and even my pyjamas were soaking wet. All I can remember is something about a very, very high bungee jump into a lake of icy cold water.'

'Well that's strange indeed Dad,' said Chelford smiling, 'that's one of the dreams I wanted to sell to Mickey Drippin. I wondered what had happened to it.'

'Da-ad,' said Chelford after a long pause, 'so you don't really know if you were dreaming or if it were real. Surely that means you are not as clever as you thought you were and, in fact, not even as clever as me?'

Confused by all that had happened Chelford's father climbed back up the stairs and looked once again in through the door of Chelford's bedroom.

There were no tins, there were no boxes and there were no jars with screw tops or bottles with corks. In fact there was nothing on the shelves at all.

On the other side of the room Chelford was fast asleep in his bed

'Now that's odd,' thought Chelford's father as he made his way back across the landing towards his bedroom followed by a trail of wet footprints.

'Have I been dreaming or not?'

From beneath the bedclothes Chelford chuckled quietly, 'there is always the dimwit who can't tell a dream from reality.'

The end

16.

Whitworth remembers something he once read in a book.

'Can you see what I see? In that field on the little island near the other bank of the river?' clucked a very excited Whitworth one sunny afternoon. 'If I am not mistaken, it looks like ears of corn swaying in the wind. Now what is a chicken's most important and favourite food my friends?'

'Corn Whitworth, fresh, succulent golden ears of corn,' clucked the chickens all at the same time.

'Corrrrrect!' replied the rather plump cockerel. 'The problem is, how do we get to the island so we can eat some of it?'

'We can't fly... well not very far anyway,' added Coughdrop.

'We could build ourselves an ark, like the one Noah built, and then we could sail across,' clucked Slimline who always had some really good ideas.

'We could try swimming, but none of us know how. We don't even like getting our feet wet!' said Britney in her rather singsong voice. 'Anyway, even if we could swim there is one itsy bitsy problem we would need to think about first.'

Whitworth, Coughdrop and Slimline all stared at Britney and waited for her to explain what this "itsy bitsy" problem actually was.

'Yes?' said Whitworth rather inquisitively. 'Yes?' he repeated loudly after a long pause.

'Well, it's the rather large crocodile floating in the water. I fear it could swallow us all up if it caught us trying to swim, or even paddle across the river. You know chickens are a crocodile's favourite meal!' clucked Britney and she pointed her wing at a rather long and scaly shape with two big black staring eyes, floating on the surface of the water.

'Hmmmmm,' clucked Whitworth looking down at the crocodile, 'I wouldn't want to get my feet wet anyway.'
After giving the problem some serious thought Whitworth suddenly had a brilliant idea.

'Why don't I ask the crocodile if he will give us a lift across the river on his back? It's the only part of him that always seems to stay above of the water.'

Coughdrop, Slimline and Britney huddled together to discuss Whitworth's plan. They quickly decided that, although it sounded quite a good idea, it would be better if Whitworth were to be the first to try it out.

'Excuse me Mr Crocodile,' crowed Whitworth from the riverbank. 'As we chickens cannot swim and haven't had time to build ourselves an ark, would you mind awfully taking me, and possibly my friends, across the river? We need to get to the little island near the opposite bank so we may eat from that field full of corn that's waving so gracefully in the wind.'

The scaley old crocodile smiled, baring all his teeth, and nodded in agreement sending little ripples of water shimmering up the river bank that made all the chickens squawk, flap and clatter as it almost made their feet wet.

'Do come aboard my feathered friend,' gargled the old crocodile, 'and stand on the end of my mouth, oops, sorry I meant nose. You will find it so much dryer at that end.'

Whitworth stood where he was told and the crocodile swished and swashed its long scaly tail back and forth and began to swim across the river.

'Once we get close to the island, little chicken,' cackled the crocodile when he was halfway across, 'I am going to open my mouth as wide as wide can be and I will swallow you whole in one gulp.'

Sure enough, as the island drew nearer and nearer the crocodile's mouth began to open wider and wider.

'Now wait just one moment before you eat me, Mr Crocodile,' whispered Whitworth into one of the crocodile's ears, 'I have just had a thought that may be of interest to you. Why don't you let me taste the corn first, and then take me back across the river? I can tell my friends, who are waiting for me on the riverbank, how wonderful it is.

I am sure they would love to return to the island with me and then you can eat them as well.'

'Hmmm,' thought the crocodile, 'now that sounds an excellent idea to me.' He closed his mouth with a resounding "snap" and waited near the island until Whitworth had filled himself full of corn.

The crocodile returned to the riverbank with Whitworth standing rather proudly on the tip of his nose, cock-a-doodle doo-ing at the top of his voice about how successful the trip had been.

Whitworth told the three hens how delicious the corn was and well worth tasting, and said they needn't worry about getting their feet wet as the crocodile had promised to take them all back over so they could eat their fill.

'Welcome aboard again my feathered friend,' gargled the old crocodile. 'If you and the three young ladies would like to shuffle down the bus towards my teeth, oops, sorry, I meant nose, you will find it a lot drier there and I will make sure that during the trip you won't even get your feet wet.'

Whitworth, Slimline, Coughdrop and Britney did exactly as they were told and stood on the very end of the crocodile's long and pointed nose.

'Once we get close to the island, little chickens,' sniggered the old crocodile when he was halfway across the river, 'I shall open my mouth as wide as wide can be and swallow you all up in one gulp.'

Sure enough as the island drew closer and closer the crocodile's mouth began to open wider and wider, even if, with all four chickens standing on the end, it did prove a little more difficult and a lot slower to open.

'Now wait just one moment before you swallow us all up Mr. Crocodile,' Whitworth quietly whispered into one of the crocodile's ears, 'I have just had a thought that may be of interest to you.

Why don't you wait until we have filled ourselves up with delicious golden corn? Then we will be as plump as plump could be. By then we will be the most delicious chickens you will ever have tasted in your life.'

'Hmmm,' thought the crocodile, 'now that does sound like an excellent idea to me.' He closed his mouth with a resounding "snap" and waited near the island as all four chickens spent the afternoon scratching and pecking at the succulent fresh golden corn.

When they were full the four friends returned to the river, climbed onto the scaley back of the old crocodile and stood where they were told to, at the end of the crocodile's nose.

'When I get close to the river bank,' chuckled the crocodile 'I am going to open my mouth as wide as wide can be and swallow you all up in one gulp.'

As they approached the bank of the river the old crocodile tried his very best to open his large mouth but failed. The weight of the cockerel, plus the three chickens all full to bursting with corn, was just far too heavy for him and his jaws stayed firmly shut.

'Why didn't the crocodile eat us all like he promised Whitworth?' asked Coughdrop as they walked away from the riverbank.

Whitworth explained to Coughdrop about how he had once read a book, which said even though a crocodile has very strong muscles for closing its mouth, it has very weak muscles for opening it.

'The weight of us four, full up with corn was just too heavy for him and as a result the crocodile couldn't open his mouth wide enough to eat us.'

'Ah!!!!!' squawked Coughdrop and Slimline at the same time.

'That's the trouble with you Whitworth, you read too many books,' clucked Britney as she made her way up the lane and back towards the farm, singing a little song and dancing from side to side.

'I have told you before you will never learn anything useful from reading books, mark my words!!!!!'

The end

17. Linfant's tale.

Linfant the shark was a rather upper class sort of fish
Who would only eat food that was served on a plate or a dish.
A red and white napkin he would tuck under his chin
Before breakfast, or dinner or even tea could begin.

Some dolphins collected and bought him a knife and a fork
And with some money left over, a film, starring Mickey Rourke.
Then one of his close friends, a whale, called Sinbad by name
Who was a clever old fish and always well ahead of the game.

Said, 'Linfant there are no dishes and plates left anymore
You have used every single one from that ship wrecked on
the ocean floor.'
It was true, for in oceans so deep and oceans so wide
Not one single plate, bowl or dish could be spied.

'I said you were wrong, you should be just enjoying the food
Because eating the dishes as well was extremely naughty... and rude.'
True, the shark would eat everything be it raw, boiled or fried
The trouble with Linfant was his mouth... It was too big and too wide.

Now Sinbad was massive, one of the biggest fish in his school
So no one in the ocean dare take him for a fool.
'You are going to have to change, Linfant, and alter your ways
You see this "eating off plates" idea is just a silly, juvenile craze.'

Then Sinbad the whale had a brilliant idea
But needed some assistance from friends far and near.
Tarquin the turtle was the first to offer some help.
And brought with him a shopping bag full of tasty brown kelp.

'We could try placing this food on top of my extremely hard back
Cos' that looks a bit like a table, a plate, dish or rack'
'What a brilliant idea,' said Sinbad, 'let's lay down a cloth
Here's his starter for lunch, it's a bowl of fish broth.'

The food was devoured in one extremely short sitting.
There was, however, one thing that wasn't quite fitting.
Tarquin had vanished, he had disappeared from view
And where he had gone, the others had not a clue.

'Now that was rather scrummy,' said Linfant licking his lips.
'Perhaps next time I eat it I'll ask for a side order of chips.'
Now even though the turtle wore an extremely hard shell.
It made little difference to Linfant, he had swallowed the tablecloth...
and Tarquin as well.

'Hey!' exclaimed Sinbad 'that's a little unfair and certainly a little unjust.
It must have been like eating a pork pie with an over cooked crust.
We need to sit down and think what next we should do.
In the meantime Linfant burped loudly and swam off to the loo.

An octopus named Oli had a super idea and thought
And one that should stop at least himself getting caught.
He could hold high the food on all tentacles eight.
With that number of supports there would be no need for a plate.

'A brilliant idea,' the friends all agreed.
But now it was time to prepare Linfant's next feed.
They made four different curries, rice puddings and jelly,
That would hopefully end up in and fill Linfant's large belly.

There was one gulp, and two gulps, and three gulps, and four.
Sinbad counted eight but there was still one gulp more?
Now Oli was missing, gone, nowhere to be seen.
'Whooooo' said the others, and their faces turned green.

The tastes and the flavours Linfant just could not fault,
Though if he made them himself he would use perhaps a little less salt.
'I've done it, I am winning, I have really made the change
Although eating without a knife, fork or plate still seems rather strange'

'Cripes,' uttered Sinbad, 'perhaps it's time I swam south.
I don't want to end up in Linfant's large mouth.'
Now whales are not known to be the fastest of creatures
But specialise in owning extremely large features.

Out of the corner of his eye the shark saw something swish.
'It must be more food,' he thought, 'as there's no sign of a dish.'
It wasn't too long before he caught up with a tail
As he snapped and he bit he caused a deafening wail.

But Sinbad had gone, he was now miles down the coast.
He had stopped at the services for some hot tea and brown toast.
So whose tail was caught and whose tail was bitten?
From the noise it was clear something had been severely smitten.

There is not a lot of this story I have left to tell,
Because after eating that tail, Linfant ate himself up as well.

The end

18. The saga of Jepson Bumford.

'Headmaster, I think we may have a problem'
Said Professor Evans one fine day.
'It's that big nosed kid, Jepson Bumford;
I can't allow him in the yard to play.

We were half way through my lesson,
Learning precisely how to spell,
When he pushed his finger up his nose
And his notebook went up as well.

I pulled and pushed and shook and tugged,
I even used this hook,
But nothing seemed to help dislodge
Either his finger or the book.

So I called on Jake the Gardener
For some help and inspiration.
He tried this and that, then that and this,
Then gave up in desperation.

Trouble began when Jake used his pick
And then his garden spade.
When he failed to remove either finger or book
Our hopes began to fade.

When we realised that both pick and spade
Were stuck up his nose as well,
We called on Ron the Caretaker,
And to him our story did tell.

He hurried over with his bag of tools,
A hammer, drill and wrench.
He said, 'it's a tricky operation, keep him still,'
So we strapped Bumford to a bench.

He hammered and chiselled, sawed and drilled
For almost three quarters of an hour.
That was when his batteries ran flat,
Ron had used up all the power.

We thought it had worked, but just about then
We suddenly ran out of luck.
Ron the Caretaker let out a deafening yell
As both his screwdriver and spanner were stuck.

We pulled him one way and then the other
And then back the same way once more.
We pulled Bumford so hard he fell off the bench
And landed on the classroom floor.'

'So it wasn't just his finger' said the Head,
'That Bumford had stuck up his nose,
There were books and tools and screwdrivers,
And did someone mention a hose?

There's no alternative, we have no choice,
We shall phone for Fireman Fred.
This could be a tricky situation;
Requiring the coolest of head.'

The bright red engine clanged through the town
And on towards the school.
Fred thought at first it was a joke,
A typical schoolboy's 'April Fool.'

The sight that greeted the fire crew
As they burst through the classroom door,
Was Jepson's nose oozing with... "things"
As he lay on the classroom floor.

Fireman Fred had a brilliant thought,
To resolve the issue would be a "breeze."
But after four large pots of the cook's best pepper
He failed to make Jepson sneeze.

'We will connect our hosepipe to his empty nostril,
Now that should do the trick,
Then turn this valve up to maximum force
And move out of the way, rather quick.'

There was a "hiss", a "whoosh", and a gurgling "zing"
Followed by a horrid "gloop",
When the headmaster did a final count
There was someone missing from the group.

At the time it didn't really matter a jot,
In fact it mattered not a tanner,
As on the floor where Jepson once lay
Was the book, some tools, and the spanner.

The Gardener and the Caretaker smiled,
They were as pleased as pleased could be.
Now they could both get back to work
Once they had brewed a fresh cup of tea.

'Now hold on here, just wait one moment,'
Uttered a rather concerned Headmaster.
'I think this little misadventure
Could turn into a major school disaster.'

'What do we do, what shall we say
To Bumford's Mum and Dad.
Surely the loss of their son Jepson
Will make them extremely sad?

I know he always picked his nose
And rolled bogies into a ball,
But losing the lad just like this
Could be bad news for one and all.

As School Headmaster it rests with me
To resolve an awkward situation.
He is still a pupil at my school
Even though he has made a, er... heavenly migration.

I need to tell his parents,
It's my duty, that's plain to see.
In fact I'd better get over to his house,
Before his Mum makes tea for three.'

It wasn't far to Jepson's home,
Down the street and around the bend.
The Headmaster wished there was an easy way
To draw this saga to an end.

He rapped on the window, hammered on the door
And ten times rang the bell.
'It's nothing really urgent, Mrs B, but your son, Jepson,
He's er... how can I put it... not feeling too well.'

'Now there's good news and some bad news,
With which would you like me to start?
I suggest we take them in reverse order,
Let's put the horse before the cart.

As I said, young Jepson, he's er... gone
And I don't think he will be back too soon.
Because if you look quite closely you can see him there,
Look..., he's orbiting the moon.

Jepson's parents both glanced skywards
And saw in the distance a tiny dot.
Mother returned to the kitchen
To turn the gas down beneath her cooking pot.

'What's he doing up there Headmaster,
Shouldn't he be with you at school?
I told him before that without education
He would end up a simple fool.'

'Maybe Fred applied too much pressure,
Perhaps a little too much force,
Jepson was laying there one minute then,
'Whoosh,' nature took its course.

He shouted something, scribbled some words
Then went skywards like a rocket.
But we did find a note that says 'I love you mum'
In this jacket pocket.

'This is all that's left, just a pair of shoes,
Oh, and is this red coat Jepson's jacket?'
If it is, we will have it cleaned for free,
So it shouldn't cost you a packet.

He could well be circling around the moon
For a decade or even more.
So you may be lucky enough to sell his coat
To a pupil in Year Four.

We all accept that nothing can be done,
There really is little hope.
So by way of compensation
We bought you a brand new telescope.

We thought that when the skies are clear
With not a cloud at all in sight,
You will be able to sit in your garden
And watch Jepson all through the night.'

'I told him more than once, Headmaster,
Jepson, please don't pick your nose.
You know it looks so awful,
And the bogies cling to your clothes.

You have tried your best Sir, we can't complain,
The truth is plain to see,
And thank you, Headmaster, for letting us know
Before Mother started making our tea.'

Each clear evening in Jepson's garden
Half way along Dingbat Street,
There is always a gathering of neighbours
Enjoying the nightly galactic treat.

Each one shouts up a message that
The Town Council would be looking into his case.
But it's doubtful he ever hears them as
He floats quietly around in space.

'I can still see him Mother, there he is,
And he's enjoying himself a treat.
He must be the only astronaut in outer space
Orbiting in stockinged feet.

I think we should be grateful,
In fact, I thing we should be proud,
That at last our young son Jepson,
Has stood out of the crowd.'

It was six or seven years later
When an important fact was found,
It was concerning some coloured asteroids
That had landed on Earthy ground.

They were round and green, some soft, some hard,
But tests proved they were of human race.
They were Jepson's rolled up bogies,
All the way from outer space.

**The end
(not quite)**

and now,
as a special treat
for getting this far…

a top secret,
sneak preview
of book 3…

19. Difference.

'What's the difference twixt a cat and a rat?'
Asked the teacher one day. 'Children, now answer me that.'
'A cat has legs at each end, and is clever and smart,'
Said Alistair Crump who was hopeless at art.

'It has a tail at the rear and whiskers at the other.'
Added the boy seated behind, who was Alistair's twin brother.
'It has two keen eyes and a very sensitive smell,'
Nodded Kitty Muldoon, 'there's not much more left to tell.'

'But a rat has four legs and is clever as well
With whiskers and tail and a nose that can smell.'
'So what is the difference I ask you once more?
Please tell me your answer, pupils in the class of year 4?

'Well?
Anyone?'

No one in the class raised a hand.

'Okay!'

'So what is the difference twixt a dog and a hog?'
Asked the teacher one day, 'it's easier than falling off a log.'
'I know,' Welsey aspired, and thrust his hand way up high.
'One lives in a kennel and the other in a sty.'

'A dog always sniffs and rummages on the ground,
Said Barnaby Catchpole, who rarely uttered a sound.
'A dog will eat anything from scraps to a joint.'
Added Milly Millander, eagerly making her point.

'Let's see,' said the teacher rubbing his chin.
'Where is the easiest place for me to begin?
Now a kennel and a sty are exactly the same.
They are made out of wood, a house, that's the aim.

A hog will forage from morning 'til night
And will also eat everything that comes into its sight.
So what is the difference I ask you once more?
Please tell me your answer, pupils in the class of year 4?

'Well?
Anyone?'

No one in the class raised a hand.

'Okay!'

'So what is the difference twixt a bike and a hike?'
Asked the teacher one day, 'here's one you should like.'
'A bike takes you places you have never before been,'
Whispered Adrian Dunkley to Annabelle Green.

'On a bike it's the legs, they go up and they go down,'
Shouted the noisy and disruptive Geraldine Brown.
'And you can travel and roam just where you please,
Up and down hills with the greatest of ease.'

'But when you hike your legs also go up and go down.
Just as we were told by Miss Geraldine Brown.
You can also walk to places you've not seen before.
So what is your final answer?' said the teacher to the pupils of year 4.

'Well?
Anyone?'

No one in the class raised a hand.

'Okay!'

'Take the 'R' out of rat and add in a 'C'
Take the 'H' from the hog and add in a 'D'
Take the 'H' out of hike and add in a 'B'
An answer to the question you should now clearly see.'

'Well?

Anyone?'

One person in the class held up his hand

'Yes?' said the teacher.

'I know the answer, I've resolved teacher's riddle,'
Shouted Wally O'Grady and he started to giggle.
'There is only one difference and the truth I am telling
They are exactly the same except for the spelling.'

'Whooo!!!' said the pupils all at the same time.

'The answers to questions are not always so hard.
Find the easy resolve but always be on your guard.
'Wally's right,' said the teacher, 'now that wasn't such a chore.
So well done to you all in the class of year 4.'

The end

20.

Primrose,
the 'Prima Ballerina'.

If there was one thing that Primrose the young hippopotamus liked to do more than anything else in the world it was to dance.

All through the years she spent at junior and senior school she was a brilliant pupil at sums, cooking and even 'gymelastics' (as her mother used to call it). In fact, according to her father 'she could well have gone on to study nuclear science at a top university'.

But, in the end, it was dancing that Primrose loved more than anything else.

She enjoyed all kinds of dance from waltzes to sambas, gavottes to rumbas. She could even dance an Irish jig. However, it was classical ballet that Primrose loved most of all. As soon as she arrived home from school in the evening she would rush to get her homework completed before setting off for a secluded clearing she knew of deep in the forest. There she would practice all her steps. As none of the animals in the jungle could play any sort of music, Primrose would hum and sing quietly to herself as she practiced all the difficult ballet movements.

One particular evening, whilst she was on her way home from school, Primrose saw a rather large signboard. It was informing all the animals in the jungle that a ballet troupe was going to perform in a village near her home. She was so excited she rushed home as fast as she could to tell her mother and father the news.

'Wouldn't it be wonderful mum if, at some time, I could dance in a ballet' she said to her mother as the family sat down for their supper.

'Well yes it would Primrose,' replied her mother, 'but most of the ballet dancers that I have seen, as well as having a pretty face are awfully small and thin. Now I know both your father and I think you are the prettiest hippopotamus on the river Chimboko, but you must admit, Primrose, you are not really small and not all that thin either. In fact, when we weighed you last week you were only a few kilograms short of two tonnes.'

Primrose felt rather disappointed and perhaps a little hurt by her mother's comments and after she finished her tea she left her home to go for a walk. She felt rather saddened and a little dejected.

'I know I can dance better than anyone else in my school,' she said to herself and a little tear, or two, rolled down her long face. 'I will show Mum and Dad how clever I am.' And she slowly started to smile once again.

It was early the following morning when Gengis, the lion, and King of the jungle, arrived in the forest clearing and summoned all the animals to listen to what he had to say.

'Now listen everyone to what I have to say,' roared Gengis. 'We have an itsy bitsy problem that needs to be sorted out. It appears that Yolando, the famous Russian ballet-dancing ostrich, is sick and the troupe has no one available to take her place. If we can't find someone soon I am afraid the ballet on Friday night will have to be cancelled.'

'To try and help them out I am proposing to organise a contest, and who-so-ever wins the contest will be allowed to dance with the troupe in the ballet. So, these are the rules' and Gengis reached for a rather thick book out of his back pocket.

'As well as being able to dance, the contestants will need to have a pretty face, must be able to either hum or sing in tune and, most importantly, they must prove to the judges that they are extremely light and agile on their feet.'

'Gamp the chimpaneze, Thrumpet the elephant and myself will be the four judges,' roared Gengis, who, although king, was not known to be brightest of the lions in the jungle when it came to adding up. 'We will look closely at each contestant's face, listen to them singing and in addition each one will need to show how light and agile they are on their feet by standing and dancing on a couple of these eggs.' Gengis held high a basket full of fresh chicken's eggs for all to see. 'We shall then give each one marks out of five,' he added holding up two 'paw fulls' of sharp claws.

Of all the different species of birds, mammals and animals that lived in the jungle only two thought they were qualified enough to enter the contest.

Tordorf the turkey and Cutlet the crocodile were the only two who wished to enter the competition. But then, just at the last moment, Primrose the hippopotamus held up her stubby little tail and asked Gengis if she could take part too...

Gengis nodded his head rather reluctantly because Primrose's request came so late. He gave the three contestants two fresh eggs each and sent them away to practice in readiness for the auditions the following evening.

Primrose did everything she could to improve her already pretty face. She also practiced her singing. But most important of all she had to prove she was lighter and more agile on her feet than any other animal in the jungle.

In the clearing the following evening, quite a crowd of animals had gathered to cheer on their favourite contestant.

'First of all, please show your support and appreciation for the crocodile,' roared Gengis. The crowd clapped and cheered as Cutlet swished his massive tail and waddled into the clearing. He smiled his best smile at the judges and began to sing his song.

When he finished there was a loud applause and everyone waited for Cutlet to start his dance.

'Where are your eggs?' shouted Thrumpet.

'Well, I was hungry whilst I was practicing my smile, so I ate them,' answered Cutlet.

Cutlet's reply was followed by a significant amount of booing from the animals assembled in the clearing.

'Ok, so it's one out of five for a pretty smile, one out of five for the song and nought out of five for being light and agile on your feet,' announced Gamp. Cutlet is in the lead with a score of two, and he chalked the number onto a piece of board.

'Next contestant is the turkey,' announced Gengis, holding up a piece of paper, and Tordorf strutted proudly into the clearing.

She opened her beak, just a little, winked at the judges and began to cluck her little song. As she clucked she placed the two eggs on the grass and carefully, but very carefully, danced around them before finally stepping onto the thin brown shells.

Just before the audience shouted 'she's done it' and were about to burst into applause there was two loud cracks. The shells had broken leaving Tordorf standing in the middle of two very messy fresh eggs.

There was a disappointing 'ohhhhhhh' from the animals before Gamp announced the scores.

'Tordorf is awarded one for the pretty face and one for the wink, (the judges quite liked that idea), making two out of five in total. She gets another two out of five for her rather high pitched, ear piercing, monotonous song, but nought out of five for being light and agile on her feet,' Gamp proclaimed. 'So the turkey is in the lead with four,' and he chalked Tordof's score up on the board.

'Next contestant is the hippopotamus,' roared Gengis for the third and last time and Primrose took a deep breath and, rather timidly, walked into the middle of the clearing.

She smiled her best smile at the judges and then began to sing and hum her special song.

'Not much of a smile, and she even has something rather gooey dripping from her mouth,' Gamp said quietly to Thrumpet.

'Her humming is so quiet that even with my large ears I still can't hear anything,' murmured Thrumpet the elephant.

'That's going to be two noughts out of five to start with,' whispered Gengis and the other two judges nodded their heads in agreement.

Primrose realised she would need full marks for being light and agile on her feet to be able to win the contest. She carefully placed the two eggs on the grass and danced her best dance ever around them before finally stepping lightly onto the shells.

The audiences gasped in horror, but, nothing happened. The shells stayed unbroken and Primrose, as an 'encore,' even did a little pirouette on one of them.

'Well bless my trunk,' trumpeted the elephant, 'we will have to award her five out of five for that. I have never in all my one hundred and fifty years in this jungle seen anyone as light as that on their feet.'

'That means Primrose has scored two noughts and a five' proclaimed Gamp 'making five in total,' and he chalked the figure onto the piece of board.

'That settles it, Primrose the hippopotamus is the winner,' roared Gengis, 'and she will perform with the troupe at the ballet on Friday night.'

Primrose smiled the widest smile ever and skipped and hopped all the way back home to tell her parents the news.

'Mother, Mother,' she shouted excitedly, 'I have just won a competition and I will be dancing with the ballet troupe on Friday night. I am going to be a "Prima Ballerina" she proclaimed proudly, and instantly went round and round on the tips of her toes.

The ballet was a huge success. All the animals that came to watch the show applauded Primrose loudly when she bowed and smiled at the final curtain call.

After the show had ended and as Primrose, who was still wearing her pretty pink dress, and her parents walked back home, her mother asked how she managed to dance on top of two eggs without breaking them.

'Quite simple mother,' she replied, 'I remembered what my cookery teacher taught me in class.

I just boiled them in water first for ten minutes.'

The end (yes, really!)

oops... sorry!!